Jon leaned closer until his mouth hovered only inches above hers

"What's behind that beautiful face of yours, Amanda Hightower?" he murmured, his tone light, but the question serious. "What are you really like?"

Her eyes, so close to his that he could see the tiny specks of gold within the rich brown, became wary. "What do you mean? I'm exactly what I appear to be."

She'd stiffened as he'd moved closer, but she didn't step away. He wondered if she was as curious as he was. He hoped so. "Oh, no, I don't think you're what you appear to be at all. I think there are a lot of surprises hidden behind that proper Southern-lady exterior." He closed the last little bit of space between them and kissed her.

She tasted better than peaches, he thought as he brushed his mouth across hers. Much better. And then need and desire took over when she began to respond, when her soft, moist lips clung to his.

Who'd have thought prim, proper, reserved Amanda Hightower could kiss like that?

Talented and popular **Gina Wilkins**
continues to delight her many fans with her
marvelous stories. Gina's many readers
especially enjoy the reappearance of
characters they met in previous novels—
it's like meeting long-lost friends.
As Luck Would Have It introduces the
Luck family, who are often under the mercy
of their well-intentioned mother. In April
1994, you'll be able to read more about them
in *Just Her Luck*.

Books by Gina Wilkins

HARLEQUIN TEMPTATION

AS LUCK WOULD HAVE IT

GINA WILKINS

Harlequin Books

TORONTO • NEW YORK • LONDON
AMSTERDAM • PARIS • SYDNEY • HAMBURG
STOCKHOLM • ATHENS • TOKYO • MILAN
MADRID • WARSAW • BUDAPEST • AUCKLAND

For Dolores Silakowski, of Parma, Ohio:
No writer could ask for a more loyal
or more encouraging reader.
Thank you—and happy birthday.

ISBN 0-373-25570-5

AS LUCK WOULD HAVE IT

Copyright © 1993 by Gina Wilkins.

Prologue

THE SMALL BOY sitting in the library's main reading room glanced at the expensive watch strapped to his thin wrist, sighed and closed the heavy volume on the table in front of him. Aubrey Jerome Hightower loved the hushed cerebral, dust-and-disinfectant-scented atmosphere of the library; he was more comfortable here than in his grandmother's east Memphis mansion where he'd been forced to live for the past five months. He rose reluctantly to go to meet Terrence, his grandmother's chauffeur, who would be arriving soon to pick him up. Mrs. Campbell, the head librarian, gave him a smile as he passed her desk. Aubrey returned it absently, intent on balancing the pile of books he clutched against his skinny chest.

A wave of heat hit him as he walked outside into the early September afternoon. The gray Lincoln wasn't parked in its usual place at the curb. Frowning, he looked up and down the busy street, his gaze skimming past the buxom blond woman heading his way. Odd. Terrence was *never* late. Grandmother simply wouldn't allow it.

"Aubrey?"

He turned his head in response to the tentative greeting, and found the blond woman standing beside him. He pushed his glasses higher on his nose and studied her through the strong lenses. "Yes?"

She smiled beneath her oversize purple sunglasses. With her round face and rather pink nose, Aubrey thought the big dark glasses made her look like a chubby blond bug. He'd never seen her before. "I'm Mona," she said in a breathy, talking-to-a-little-kid manner that Aubrey found annoying. "I'm a friend of your aunt Amanda's, and I'm here to take you home."

He took an instinctive step backward. "Why?"

She giggled. "Now don't get excited. Terrence is running an errand for your grandmother, so your aunt asked me to pick you up. I was on my way over for a visit, anyway, so I said I'd be happy to. You don't mind, do you, sweetie?"

Aubrey was only nine years old and small for his age, but he hated it when someone talked to him as though he were a slow-witted child. He wasn't, of course. He was extremely advanced for his age, which was why he knew there was something peculiar about this encounter. Security-conscious, routine-bound Grandmother would *never* send Terrence on an errand when she knew he was expected to drive Aubrey home.

Holding his books more tightly, he took another step back toward the security of the library. "I'll call Aunt Amanda just to make sure it's okay," he said, trying to sound calm and confident. "There's a phone in the library."

The blond's smile dimmed perceptibly, though she made a visible effort to hold on to it. "Aubrey, dear, I admire your common sense, but we really don't have time for that right now. I promised your aunt Amanda I'd have you home in time for tea. You know how Roseanne resents it when her wonderful little afternoon snacks get cold or stale."

Aubrey didn't understand how this woman knew so much about the Hightower household, but he was not getting into a car with her without authorization from his aunt. There was something about her he didn't trust. "I'll make it quick," he promised, turning toward the library door as he spoke. "Be right back."

She reached out to stop him. "Now that's enough of this nonsense!" she said taking the tone of an annoyed schoolteacher. "Get in the car, Aubrey."

He dodged out of reach of her long-nailed fingers. "No!" he shouted and broke into a run.

She snatched at him again, this time catching a bit of his sleeve and jerking him backward. He stumbled, but broke free and without looking back, he pushed past a flustered woman balancing a baby, two library books, a purse and a diaper bag. "Be careful!" the young mother said sharply.

Aubrey hardly even heard her as he pushed open the library door. All he heard was the voice of the blond, calling his name and demanding that he stop. His heart pounding in his throat, he took a breath of relief when he was safely inside. He risked a look out through the glass in the door. The blond stood just outside, looking indecisive. Her head turned one way and then another, her chubby hands clenched and unclenched at her sides. And then her mouth moved—Aubrey could just imagine the word she'd snarled—and she turned and hurried away, almost at a run.

He sagged against the door, blinking rapidly behind his glasses, reminding himself that exceptionally bright nine-year-old boys didn't cry when they were upset. Grandmother said so.

"Aubrey? Dear, is something wrong? Where is Terrence?"

Aubrey started at the voice, then turned quickly to Mrs. Campbell. He would have liked to have thrown himself into her comforting-looking arms, but the Hightowers were not so demonstrative. "I think we should call the police, Mrs. Campbell," he said, straightening his shoulders and drawing himself up to his full four feet two inches. "I believe someone just tried to kidnap me."

1

AMANDA HIGHTOWER SHIFTED her weight in the fragile, uncomfortable antique French chair, closed her eyes and allowed herself thirty full seconds to fantasize about a sun-drenched beach. The warm sand and sparkling water she pictured could have been in Hawaii or Tahiti or Jamaica, anywhere but the fussy front parlor of the gracefully aging Hightower family mansion in the old-money section of Memphis, Tennessee. "Mental mini-vacations," she called these daydreams, which sometimes gave her strength when the pressures of real life became too much to handle. Like now.

Reluctantly she opened her eyes and focused on the frowning face of her mother, Eleanor Cummings Hightower. Eleanor had been talking for the past ten minutes, unaware that her daughter's thoughts had wandered so far while she'd droned on. Amanda made a determined effort to concentrate on her mother's angry monologue, which was directed toward what Eleanor considered to be the incompetence and indifference of the Memphis Police Department.

One more time Amanda tried halfheartedly to defend the local boys in blue, though she was beginning to agree with her mother that they hadn't been as helpful as they could have been. She tried to calm Eleanor by saying, "The police have done all they can for now, Mother. They simply have no other clues to pursue."

Eleanor's gray eyes snapped behind her designer eyeglasses. "What else do they need?" she demanded. "Aubrey gave them an excellent description of the woman who tried to kidnap him, down to each article of clothing she was wearing, and still those rude so-called detectives said it wasn't enough. Did they expect a nine-year-old boy to grab his would-be abductor and hold her until they arrived to take over?"

"Mother, there must be hundreds of chubby blondes in Memphis—thousands. The police can't question all of them. As they pointed out, they don't even know for certain the woman *was* a blond. She was probably wearing a wig. They have no description of a car, no testimony of witnesses.... There's nothing else they can do."

In an uncharacteristic display of emotion, Eleanor tapped one thin pale fist against the arm of her chair and raised her voice. "A woman tried to kidnap my grandson two days ago, and the police tell me there is nothing more they can do about it! I'm supposed to just accept that without protest?"

For once, Amanda found herself in full sympathy with her mother. She, too, was horrified by what had almost occurred and by the possibility that another attempt to kidnap Aubrey might be made, but she was realistic enough to know that help wouldn't come from the Memphis Police Department. Not without more clues than they had at this point.

"We're not going to just sit back and let someone take Aubrey, Mother," she said firmly, injecting as much confidence as she could into her voice. "We'll take steps to make sure he's protected from now on. No more unsupervised visits to the library or the museum. Someone will be with him at all times. If it will make you feel better, we'll hire a private investigator to look into the incident, though I doubt he'd get any further than the police have."

Eleanor crossed her hands in her lap, looking just a bit smug, which made Amanda suspicious.

"Mother? What have you done?"

"I've already acquired the services of a security expert," Eleanor replied. "He'll be arriving tomorrow."

"A security expert? *What* security expert? And arriving from where?"

"From Seattle. I was talking to my old dear friend Jessica Luck yesterday, and when I told her what almost happened, she suggested we have her son come and stay with us for a few days to advise us on ways to protect Aubrey. He has experience in this sort of thing."

Though she'd never met her, Amanda had been hearing about Eleanor's old school friend Jessica Luck all her life. She knew her mother was very fond of the woman, with whom she'd kept in touch for years through letters and the occasional telephone call. But what was *this*?

She lifted both hands, in a gesture of strained patience. "All right, Mother, start from the beginning. Who is Jessica Luck's son, why does he have experience in this sort of thing, and why is he coming to stay with us?"

DETECTIVE JONATHAN LUCK swallowed a curse as he tried vainly to settle his injured leg more comfortably in the cramped space provided for the airplane's coach passengers. The pretty brunette attendant who'd been so friendly since he'd boarded in Seattle leaned over him with a concerned smile. "Mr. Luck? Are you all right? Can I get you anything?"

He shook his head. "Thanks," he added, giving her an absent smile. She lingered another moment before moving on to her duties. Though normally he would have done everything he could to become better acquainted with such an attractive—and obviously attracted—woman, Jon didn't try to detain her. He was too damned uncomfortable, and too angry with himself for being here in the first place.

It was all his mother's fault. Why on earth had he allowed her to talk him into this?

But even as the question crossed his mind, he knew the answer. Once Jessie Luck set her mind to something, few people could dissuade her, including her adoring husband and three often exasperated, but equally adoring offspring.

"After all, Jon, you *are* on leave for the next six weeks," Jessie had reminded him unnecessarily. "And you are experienced at dealing with this sort of thing. My friend needs you, darling. You'll do this one little favor for your mother, won't you?"

It was a question he'd been hearing all his life, and one he *always* fell for. And almost without fail he'd find himself regretting his gullibility long before her not-so-little "favors" were handled to her satisfaction. But not this time, he'd decided. "No, Mother. Absolutely not," he'd answered firmly. "I'm sorry, but this time I'm going to have to refuse. There's nothing I can do for your friend, whatever her problem may be. I will *not—*"

But he had, of course. He was sitting in an airplane en route to Memphis, Tennessee, on his way to the home of two women he'd never met in his life to offer his services in protecting a nine-year-old boy who'd apparently been the target of a failed kidnapping attempt three days ago.

This one's going to be the last favor, Mom.

AMANDA PAUSED outside the closed door of her nephew's bedroom late Saturday morning, slid her open palms down the front of her full-skirted casual dress, then took a deep breath and tapped twice on the door. "Aubrey? It's Aunt Amanda."

"Come in." The young voice was muffled by the heavy wooden door, but even through that obstacle, Amanda heard his lack of enthusiasm. A tiny sigh escaped her as she turned the knob, though she pasted on a smile as she entered the room.

Aubrey was sitting at the big desk in one corner of the large bedroom, looking very small and vulnerable behind a stack of heavy textbooks. He looked up at her through his glasses, his expression courteous, but distant. As usual.

"It's almost time for lunch, Aubrey. You need to put away your books now and wash up."

He nodded and obediently closed the book in front of him. Aubrey was always obedient. "Yes, Aunt Amanda. I'll be right down."

Aubrey was always polite, too. Painfully so, Amanda thought with a touch of sadness. She started to turn away, then couldn't resist pausing another moment. "What are you studying?"

"Algebra." Aubrey was three years ahead of other schoolchildren his own age, already taking junior-high classes.

"I always liked algebra," she commented. "It's rather fun trying to find the value of x or y or whatever, isn't it? Like working a puzzle or solving a mystery."

"Yes, ma'am," Aubrey replied without looking up from the notebooks and pencils he was neatly putting away.

So much for that conversation. She took care phrasing her next question. "Aubrey... are you all right? You're not still worrying about what happened at the library the other day, are you?"

She knew Aubrey had had at least one bad dream since the incident; she'd found him restless and quietly moaning in his bed when she'd given in to the urge to check on him during the night after the attempted kidnapping. He'd denied any memory of the dream when she'd gently wakened him to offer comfort, but she knew he'd been frightened by what had happened. If only he would allow her close enough to reassure him...

"I'm fine, Aunt Amanda. I'll go wash up now. I'll see you at lunch."

He'd dismissed her as easily and as effectively as his grandmother could have—and often did. Unable to speak because of the sudden lump in her throat, Amanda nodded and left his room. And she found herself fighting tears as she walked toward her own room, a reaction that was all too common after one of her rejected attempts to get closer to the nephew who'd become her ward five months ago.

LATER THAT AFTERNOON, Amanda nervously paced the front parlor as she awaited Jonathan Luck's arrival. Her path was erratic because she had to keep dodging delicate chairs and intricately carved little tables that held fragile expensive knickknacks. She thought wistfully of the apartment she'd had to give up five months earlier. Her place had been decorated in a spare modern style that left plenty of room for pacing. Though her mother had hated it, Amanda had really liked that apartment.

But no use fantasizing now, she reminded herself sternly. It had taken the death of her brother and his wife to make her move back into her mother's house, and she had to face her responsibility to the child who had become her ward as a result of that tragedy. Amanda intended to make sure Aubrey remained safe, even if it meant hiring a full-time bodyguard to protect him. She might have already done so had her mother not convinced her to wait until after they'd talked to the so-called security expert who was due to arrive any minute.

"Security expert," she muttered, picking up a frilly throw pillow and fluffing it with more force than necessary. "Just because he's the son of an old friend of Mother's, she thinks he's an expert."

What he was, in fact, was a police detective. And the frustration she'd experienced in the three days since the kidnapping attempt, had left Amanda with no further use for cops. She wanted someone who didn't care about rules, regulations, formalities or procedures. Someone who cared about keeping Aubrey safe, whatever it took.

The discreet chime of the doorbell brought her pacing to an abrupt end. Instead of waiting for Roseanne, she turned toward the door to answer the summons herself. She'd learned, while dealing with the police, it was best to always be the one in control, even when it was something as subtle as granting admission to her home.

The man standing on the other side of the door wasn't at all what she'd expected.

Her mother had told her that Jonathan Luck was a detective in Seattle, that he'd been injured recently and would be on medical leave from his work for several weeks. Eleanor had also mentioned that thirty-three-year-old Jonathan had never married, was the oldest of three siblings and was "devoted" to his mother.

Amanda had pictured a quiet, scholarly-looking man, much like her image of Sherlock Holmes, and in precarious health. Someone who'd blend quite nicely in the Hightower household, make a few security suggestions, and then, if she was lucky, go on his way, leaving hardly a ripple in his wake.

She hadn't thought he'd be so big, so solid, so dauntingly muscular. Even the cane gripped tightly in his right hand didn't detract from the overall sense of barely-restrained power that emanated from him.

She hadn't expected a roughly handsome face that looked as though it had come in close contact with more than a few angry fists. Or thick dark brown hair that lay shaggily around his face and touched his collar in the back. Or emerald-green eyes that mirrored a smile even as they seemed to assess her in one fleeting comprehensive glance. Or a mouth that tilted into an intriguingly crooked, utterly male grin that made even Amanda's well-guarded libido surge into awareness.

To put it bluntly, she hadn't expected a man who looked as though he'd be as comfortable in a barroom brawl as he'd be in a woman's bedroom.

Honestly, Mother, what have you gotten us into?

Belatedly she remembered her manners. It was with some difficulty that she managed a polite smile. "You must be Detective Luck. I'm Amanda Hightower. Please come in."

"Just call me Jon," he said as he limped past her into the entryway. "I'm on leave."

He was followed by Terrence, a dark-skinned young man, carrying a battered leather bag in each hand.

"Terrence, will you take Mr. Luck's bags to the blue guest room?" Amanda asked.

The chauffeur nodded. "Yes, ma'am." He smiled at Jonathan as he moved toward the huge curving stairway rising up from the foyer. "See you around, Jon."

Amanda's eyebrows lifted at the familiarity, but Jonathan only returned the smile and answered, "I'm looking forward to having you show me Beale Street at night. Just let me know when you've got an evening off to go."

"You bet." Whistling an old blues number, Terrence disappeared up the stairway.

Amanda turned again to Jonathan, who looked blandly back at her, as though daring her to comment on his friendliness with the chauffeur. She felt herself bristling at the implied challenge, then decided she was still overreacting. "You make friends quickly, Detective Luck," was all she said.

"Jon," he reminded her. "And yeah, I do. When I like someone."

Before she could help it, Amanda found herself envisioning being liked by this big, sexy, rather dangerous-looking man. She suppressed an odd quiver of response to the mental image, cleared her throat and gestured toward the front parlor. "Let's sit down and get comfortable, shall we? Would you like something to drink before we start discussing my nephew's security?"

"Sounds good. It's a long trip from Seattle to Memphis," he admitted, leaning heavily on the cane as he followed her into the parlor.

She wondered if he'd been hurt in the line of duty. Her mother had said only that he'd been wounded and needed a few weeks to recover. Jonathan Luck looked like a man who rarely followed the safest paths. She urged him to be seated on the curvy Victorian sofa, which looked ridiculously small beneath him. Telling him she'd be right back, she escaped to the kitchen to summon Roseanne.

She paused for a moment in the hallway to regain her composure, which had been rather shaky ever since Jonathan Luck had turned his crooked lazy smile on her.

JONATHAN WATCHED Amanda leave the room, noting the slight sway of her slender hips, the way her full skirt flared softly around long, nicely shaped legs. *Not bad*, he thought with a lift of one eyebrow. *Not bad at all*.

Nothing about this visit was what he'd expected.

He hadn't expected to be met at the airport by a uniformed chauffeur driving a massive gray Lincoln. He'd found himself staring as Terrence had guided the car through the open gates of a sweeping estate of green lawns, colorful flower beds and massive old trees. Jon estimated the grounds covered some twelve acres. The Hightower house, a huge, redbrick, white-trimmed Colonial mansion at the end of a long driveway, had to be twenty thousand square feet.

"*This* is the Hightower residence?" he'd asked the driver, with whom he'd already felt comfortable enough to be on nickname basis.

"Nice place, huh?"

"I guess you could say that," Jon had agreed dryly. "Especially if you grew up in a three-bedroom frame house in a working-class Seattle neighborhood."

"Or a tenement house in old downtown Memphis," Terry had added soberly. "I was scared half to death first day I worked here."

Jon hadn't been particularly comfortable with the knowledge that he'd be staying here for the next week or so, but damned if he'd admit it, even to Terry. Though he'd never mingled socially with the rich crowd, he'd known plenty of them over the years, and he'd discovered that it took a lot more than money to earn his respect.

If the Hightowers had expected him to be a high-browed preppy type who'd fit right in to this high-toned formal atmosphere, they were in for a big disappointment, Jon had thought as he'd made his way rather painfully up the long flight of stairs that led to the front door of the mansion.

Jon's mother had told him that Amanda Hightower had never married, lived with her mother and nephew in the old family home and owned a little gift shop in the wealthy part of town. He'd pictured a subdued, rigidly proper spinster of approximately his own age. He hadn't been looking forward to meeting her.

And then Amanda had opened the door.

His first thought was that if this was a maid, he heartily approved of the Hightowers' taste in employees.

And then she'd smiled and spoken to him with an accent as richly Southern as his mother's recipe for

Karo-nut pie, and he'd realized how wrong his precon-
ceptions of about Amanda Hightower had been. He'd
taken in the details of her appearance in one approving
comprehensive survey: shoulder-length deep auburn
hair, heart-shaped face, wide-set dark brown eyes,
slightly tip-tilted nose, soft sweetly curved mouth,
slender but decidedly feminine figure. She looked to be
in her midtwenties and at least ten inches shorter than
his own six two.

So this was Amanda Hightower, he'd thought—
hardly the rigid spinster he'd envisioned. She was
breathtaking. Something else Mom hadn't mentioned.

A sound from the doorway made him look up in anticipation. Amanda gave him a polite smile as she came
back into the room. She walked like a lady, he noted,
but with a seductive grace that had all his male hor-
mones leaping to attention.

Okay, Mom. Maybe I'll forgive you, after all, he
thought, and decided the next few days might be much
more interesting than he'd expected.

AS SHE TOOK HER SEAT, Amanda couldn't help noticing
that Jonathan looked large and dark and utterly male
in contrast to the room's rather fussy, unarguably feminine accoutrements. The old bull-in-a-china-shop cli-
ché ran through her mind, but she dismissed it
immediately. Jonathan Luck wasn't a bull; he was more
a big, maned lion, arrogantly surveying his surroundings.

Mentally chiding herself for being fanciful, she selected a chair close enough to him to make conversa-

tion comfortable, yet far enough away for her own comfort. "Roseanne will have our refreshments ready shortly, Jonathan."

"Call me Jon," he said again, his voice a low growl that matched her leonine fancies. "If we're going to be living together, there's no need to be so formal."

She hoped he didn't notice that her cheeks warmed a bit at his use of the term "living together." He hadn't meant anything by it, of course, but for some reason she found herself listening for sexual innuendo from this man. Must be those wickedly glinting emerald eyes, she decided. "All right, Jon," she said evenly. "And please feel free to call me Amanda."

He nodded. "Why don't you tell me what makes you think someone is trying to kidnap your nephew?" he suggested.

Not a man to waste much time with social niceties, apparently. Something about the way he spoke reminded her of the frustrating, occasionally infuriating, attitude of the officers who had done so little to ensure Aubrey's safety. "I don't *think* someone tried to kidnap my nephew," she answered precisely, intending to keep the upper hand with this particular officer from the beginning. "I *know* someone did."

He nodded with a touch of impatience. "All right, don't get defensive. I just want you to tell me what happened."

Her chin lifted. "I'm *not* getting defensive. But I'm growing very tired of police implications that we're being paranoid or hysterical about Aubrey's safety. This was not a random kidnapping attempt, Detective

Luck. The woman who tried to take Aubrey called him by name and knew more about this household than she should have known. Does that sound like a random kidnapping attempt?"

He looked at her with a lifted eyebrow and answered mildly, "I didn't say it was. And you *are* being defensive, Amanda. All I did was ask a question."

She flushed at the accuracy of his words—and at the barely veiled amusement behind them. She was thoroughly fed up with the police treating her and her mother like slow-witted overemotional females.

Calling on all the dignity Eleanor had instilled in her over the years, despite her resistance, she straightened her shoulders and spoke coolly. "Three days ago, someone tried to snatch my nephew for reasons I can't begin to imagine. The police asked dozens of questions and filled out dozens of reports, but other than that they've been of very little assistance. We were advised to be 'a bit more careful' in the future and to 'try to put this behind us.' When I expressed concern that the kidnapper would try again, I was politely accused of being paranoid. So perhaps I am being a touch defensive, Detective Luck, but I think I have good reason to be!"

Jon leaned forward, his forearms braced on his thighs as he looked at her with a grim intensity that had her breath catching in her throat. "Okay, let's get a few things straight," he said, the words clipped. "First, I'm not here on an official investigation, so you can stop calling me 'Detective.' As I said, the name is Jon.

"Second, I'm not with the Memphis police, so you can stop blaming me for whatever they did to annoy you. And finally, I've come halfway across the country as a favor to my mother and yours, and if I'm going to accomplish anything while I'm here, I'm going to need some cooperation on your part, even if all that involves is answering the same questions the local officers have already asked. Think you can manage that?"

Amanda swallowed a groan, realizing that they hadn't gotten off to the best start and that the fault was mostly hers. He was right, of course—he was here to help, not to harass her. And if his mother was anything like hers, he'd probably been roped into coming. Even if there was nothing he could do—and she couldn't imagine what an injured detective from another part of the country could do that the local officers couldn't—he was a guest in the house and deserved to be treated courteously.

"I'm sorry," she said, forcing the words past the tightness in her throat. "You're right, of course. I was taking my frustration with the local police out on you, and it was unjust of me. I'm grateful, of course, that you've come to—"

"Look," he broke in with a silencing wave of one hand, "you probably didn't have any more to do with my being here than I did. If your mother's anything like mine, this was all arranged before it was even mentioned to you."

Hearing her own thoughts echoed so eerily startled her into a weak smile. "Well . . ."

"That's what I thought. Okay, here's the deal. You cooperate by repeating everything you told the Memphis officers, and I'll try not to act too much like a cop when I ask questions. I'll take a couple of days to look over your security measures and make some recommendations on beefing them up. If, by some slim chance, I get a lead on whoever might have been behind the snatch, I'll pass the information on to the local boys. After that, I'm out of here and you can get back to whatever you'd planned to do before our mothers got this brilliant idea to call me in. Fair enough?"

Disarmed by his frankness, she nodded. She opened her mouth to agree verbally, but was interrupted when a heavy-hipped woman with elaborately curled frosted hair pushed a tea cart into the room. Grateful for the temporary respite from her disconcerting guest, Amanda said quickly, "Roseanne, this is Mr. Luck, our guest for the next few days. Mr. Luck, our housekeeper, Mrs. Roseanne Wallace."

Jon had already struggled to his feet, rather to Amanda's surprise. Leaning on the cane, he gave Roseanne a warm smile. "Nice to meet you, Mrs. Wallace. Those cakes look great, especially after that airplane food I had for lunch."

Roseanne was immediately captivated, and Amanda was startled that the man who'd been so curt with her could be so charmingly smooth with the housekeeper. "Thank you, Roseanne," she said. "I'll serve. We'll let you know if we need anything else."

Alone again with Jon, she poured him a glass of iced tea and filled a small plate with sandwiches and rich tea cakes. She set the plate on the coffee table in front of him, then settled back into her chair with a glass of tea and a silent vow to be on her best behavior with him from now on.

Jon had apparently made a similar decision. "This is really good," he said, after swallowing half a sandwich in one bite.

"There are more if you like."

He nodded. "You talk, I'll eat. Start from the beginning."

Okay, so even on his best behavior Jon Luck tended to be rather curt. She could handle that without getting defensive again, Amanda told herself firmly.

Holding her glass in both hands, she took a moment to organize her thoughts before beginning. "It happened at approximately four o'clock Wednesday afternoon. Aubrey was at the public library doing some research for a school project. He'd been there for an hour and a half."

"He was there alone?" Jon asked, glancing up from his plate.

Don't get defensive, Amanda. "Yes. Terrence drove him there and was to pick him up at four by the front steps. The head librarian, Mrs. Campbell, knew he was there and was keeping an eye on him."

"A librarian is not a baby-sitter," a man's voice growled from the doorway to the parlor. "And neither is a chauffeur. Aubrey *was* alone at that library, just like he always is—and he was almost kidnapped because of the negligence of his so-called guardian. This just proves what I've been saying all along—Amanda Hightower should never have been made responsible for a nine-year-old boy!"

2

REACTING INSTINCTIVELY to the belligerence in the un-expected arrival's voice, Jon set down his plate and reached for his cane. As he gripped the smooth wooden handle, he looked from Amanda's startled stricken face to the man who stood in the doorway glaring at her with visible malice. Jon didn't know who the guy was, but he decided right then that he didn't like him.

"Howard," Amanda said as she rose to face the heavyset, balding man whom Jon judged to be in his late forties. "I didn't hear the doorbell."

"I didn't ring it," he snapped. "You've probably given orders to that overbearing housekeeper of yours to re-fuse to admit me, so I let myself in. I want to talk to you, and you're damned well going to listen this time."

Cursing his awkwardness, Jon forced himself to his feet, aware of how much less formidable he was with the cane. His voice was cold and challenging as he said, "This guy is obviously trespassing, Amanda. Would you like him to leave?"

The man she'd called Howard looked with scorn at the cane in Jon's right hand. "You're going to throw me out?"

"If I have to," Jon replied levelly, hoping he wouldn't be forced to follow through on the bluff.

"Forget it. I'm not leaving. I've got business with this woman, and unless you're a cop or an attorney, there's no need for you to be here."

Jon smiled unpleasantly. "Then I suppose it's fortunate I just happen to be a cop, isn't it?"

"Prove it."

Jon reached for his wallet.

Amanda lifted her hand. "He doesn't have to prove anything. *You're* the intruder here, Howard. What do you want?"

"I just found out today what happened at the library Wednesday. I had to hear it through the grapevine, since neither you nor your mother bothered to notify me that my nephew was almost kidnapped. You didn't think I had a right to know?"

"I tried to call you Wednesday evening," Amanda replied evenly. "You were out of town."

"I've been back in Memphis for nearly thirty-six hours."

"Obviously I didn't know your itinerary. I'm sorry you heard about the incident through gossip, Howard, but I assure you you weren't deliberately excluded."

Howard's lip curled. "Yeah, right."

Jon watched as Amanda drew a deep breath and struggled for patience. He suspected she spent a lot of time controlling a temper that was an encumbrance to her. He'd always preferred women with spirit.

"Let me introduce our houseguest, Howard," she said at length, her voice admirably calm. "This is Detective Jonathan Luck of the Seattle Police Department. He's here to assist us in taking measures to protect Aubrey. Jon, this is Aubrey's maternal uncle, Howard Worley."

Jon didn't bother to extend a hand, nor did Worley. "Seattle police?" Worley repeated, looking from Jon to Amanda. "What the hell is a Seattle cop doing giving security advice in Memphis?"

"Jon is a longtime friend of the family," Amanda replied, fudging the truth without blinking. "He's an expert at this sort of thing. I assure you, Howard, we're taking every precaution to keep Aubrey safe."

"Like leaving him alone at the public library for an hour and a half?" Worley sneered.

Amanda flinched, but answered evenly, "That won't happen again. From now on, someone will be with him at all times."

"When are you going to admit that you aren't prepared to deal with this responsibility, Amanda? Send the boy to me. Loretta and I will make sure he's safe and well cared for."

Worley's voice grew calmer and more persuasive as he continued, "You're a young single woman. You had your own life before the tragedy that took your brother and my sister—your own career, your own apartment, an engagement to a brilliant university professor. There's no need for you to give all that up because your brother irresponsibly named you as his son's guardian."

Amanda's face went pale except for two spots of color burning high on her cheeks, the only sign that her temper was struggling to get away from her. When she spoke, her voice was icy. "My brother never did anything irresponsible in his entire life, Howard. Though he didn't discuss it with me at the time, I'm sure he had very good reasons for naming me as his son's guardian. I've willingly accepted that responsibility. I have not given up my career, and the end of my engagement to Edward Miller had nothing to do with Aubrey.

"Thank you for your concern, but Aubrey will be staying here, with Mother and me. You're welcome to visit whenever you like, of course, but I would appreciate your letting us know in advance when you'll be here, as a matter of common courtesy."

Jon had to admire the way she put the guy in his place. Her rather regal tone had irritated the hell out of him earlier, but it was just what this jerk deserved.

Worley didn't appear to share Jon's admiration for Amanda's aplomb. His gray eyes narrowed and his heavy brows drew together in a petulant scowl. "I'd regret having to embarrass all of us by turning this into an ugly court battle, Amanda, but if that's what I have to do to guarantee Aubrey's welfare, I will."

She stiffened. "Are you threatening to sue for Aubrey's custody?"

"That's exactly what I'm threatening. Think about it, Amanda. My wife and I are offering the boy a normal stable home. You're a single woman living with an aging mother and a couple of hired servants who don't really care about the kid. He has no friends, and isn't involved in sports or any other activity for a boy his age. You're trying to turn him into a pampered, prissy bookworm just like—"

He stopped abruptly, but Amanda finished the sentence for him. "Like his father?"

"Like his father," Howard repeated. "Give him to me and let me turn him into a normal kid—if it's not already too late."

"I want you to leave now, Howard."

From the faint tremor in her low voice, Jon judged that Amanda wouldn't be able to control her temper much longer. He rather looked forward to seeing her lose it. Something told him she'd chew Worley into little pieces without even pausing for breath. He was almost disappointed when Worley didn't seem inclined to hang around long enough to confirm Jon's prediction.

"You haven't heard the end of this, Amanda," Worley growled, backing out of the room.

"Please, Howard. Try to avoid the dramatic clichés, will you? They make one look so foolish if one isn't careful, don't you agree?"

Point for Amanda, Jon thought with a stifled grin.

Howard gave her a look of pure venom over his shoulder as he left the room. Amanda stood still until she heard the front door slam. Only then did she allow herself to relax, though so slightly that Jon noticed only because he was watching her so closely. "I'm sorry," she said, turning back to him. "That was unpleasant."

"Has he been making a nuisance of himself ever since your brother's death?"

"As you heard, he resents very strongly that Jerome named me as Aubrey's guardian."

"Did your brother leave a sizable estate to his son, by any chance?"

She looked troubled. "Yes," she admitted. "Very sizable. Still, I don't want to believe that money is the only reason Howard wants custody of his nephew."

Jon snorted skeptically. "Why do I find it hard to believe that Worley is motivated only by the urgings of his tender heart?"

Amanda managed a weak smile. "I'm afraid I can't believe that, either." She shook her head, as though shaking off the unpleasantness of the visit, and motioned toward the couch. "Please sit back down, Jon. I'm sorry I've kept you standing on your injured leg. I was afraid to offer Howard a seat for fear he would stay longer than he did."

"I don't blame you." Jon eased himself back down onto the hard, straight-backed sofa, wondering wryly if it had been designed with maximum discomfort in mind. What he wouldn't give for the worn leather couch in his own apartment right now!

He waited until Amanda was reseated before trying one more time to find out what had happened to her nephew. "About what happened Wednesday—"

He didn't know which of them was more frustrated when they were interrupted yet again, this time by the arrival of a silver-haired woman and a skinny little boy. Eleanor and Aubrey, Jon presumed.

He struggled to his feet one more time, deciding then and there that he and his mother were going to have a very long talk when he got home. Next time she volunteered his services to one of her friends, she could just damned well figure out a way to *un*volunteer him!

"WAS THAT HOWARD WORLEY I saw leaving as I drove in?" Eleanor demanded before Amanda had a chance to greet her.

Amanda nodded. "Yes."

"What was he doing here? Did you tell him what happened?"

"He'd already heard. He was here to—" Amanda glanced at her nephew, then at Jon before continuing smoothly, "—check on Aubrey. He was quite concerned."

Eleanor harrumphed. Jon noted that Aubrey's expression didn't even waver.

Amanda went on hastily, "Mother, this is Jonathan Luck. Jonathan, my mother, Eleanor Hightower."

Eleanor studied Jon intently. "You have your mother's eyes," she said after a moment.

"So I hear," Jon answered, mildly amused by her crisp no-nonsense tone. His mother *had* mentioned that Eleanor had always been "just a teensy bit bossy." "My mother sends her best, Mrs. Hightower."

"How thoughtful. And you may call me Eleanor," she responded in the manner of royalty granting a favor to a fortunate subject. Amanda came by her airs honestly, it appeared. "This is my grandson, Aubrey Jerome Hightower. Aubrey, say hello to Mr. Luck."

Jon turned his attention to the boy standing quietly at his grandmother's side, his thin arms clutching a violin case and a leather satchel that presumably held his music books. "Hello, Mr. Luck," Aubrey recited dutifully. "It's very nice to meet you."

As he returned the greeting, Jon had to remind himself that the boy was just nine. He looked small for his age, but bore himself with a dignity that seemed odd for a kid. His short sandy hair was neatly combed, his blue eyes were somewhat enlarged by the lenses of his wire-framed glasses and his mouth curved into a smile that held little enthusiasm. He wore a crisply pressed blue plaid shirt tucked into sharply creased gray slacks, and a small pair of loafers. With tassels. Jon wondered if the kid even owned a pair of jeans and sneakers.

"How was your music recital, Aubrey?" Amanda asked. Jon thought he detected a rather tentative note in her voice, as though she wasn't quite sure how to communicate with her nephew. Aubrey had been living with her for five months. Hadn't she learned how to talk to him during that time?

"It was a good recital," Aubrey answered with no change of expression. "The audience applauded, and my teacher said I played very well."

"I'm sorry I had to miss this one. Would you like a cake? I'll have Roseanne bring you a glass of milk to go with it."

"No, thank you, Aunt Amanda. I'm really not hungry."

"Why don't you take your things up to your room, Aubrey," Eleanor suggested, taking the chair closest to Amanda's. Jon was grateful to be able to return to his own seat, uncomfortable though it was. His leg was aching. Still, he couldn't seem to pull his attention away from Aubrey. Something about the boy bothered him.

"Yes, ma'am," Aubrey replied, turning toward the doorway. "I think I'll study for a while before dinner," he added.

"Very well. But don't let the time get away from you. You don't want to be late for dinner again."

"I won't, Grandmother."

Jon watched Amanda as her nephew left the room. She seemed to have a rather strained relationship with her ward. Why? Had Worley been right about her unsuitability—perhaps even her reluctance—to serve as the boy's guardian? Had she fought the man more out of stubbornness than genuine affection for the boy? The thought made him frown.

He waited until he was sure Aubrey was gone before asking, "Does he know why I'm here?"

"Yes, of course," Amanda answered, her eyes clearing as they turned back in his direction. "We told him you're a police officer, that you have experience in security matters and that you're here to advise us about ensuring his safety."

"Is he always so . . . subdued, or is he still frightened about the kidnapping?" Jon was looking at Amanda when he asked the question, and he didn't miss the way her eyes darkened and her mouth tightened—as though he'd unwittingly touched a nerve.

But it was Eleanor who answered him. "Aubrey is a very well-behaved child, Jonathan. A brilliant boy. He's already taking seventh-grade classes—three years ahead of his age group. He's a delicate boy, has been ever since an illness he had as a baby, but he's very mature. He does have a rather serious nature, but he seems to be handling the situation well enough."

Jon wasn't at all sure he agreed, but she was the boy's grandmother, after all. She knew the kid better than he did. Most nine-year-old boys Jon knew would have dived into the cake tray face first, and he couldn't imagine any of them actually *choosing* to study—on a Saturday afternoon, no less.

Eleanor turned to Amanda. "Now that Aubrey is gone, tell me why Howard Worley was here. I'm sure there was more to his visit than concern about Aubrey."

"You're right," Amanda agreed with a slight sigh. "He insisted again that Aubrey should be living with him and used the kidnapping attempt as evidence that I'm an unfit guardian."

"How dare he? Of all the—"

"Mother," Amanda interrupted wearily, "I've already had to ask Howard to give up the dramatic clichés. Please, don't you start."

Jon almost choked swallowing an appreciative chuckle. So, Amanda was no more cowed by her officious mother than she had been by him or Worley. Good for her.

Eleanor frowned. "Really, Amanda," she chided. "There's no need to be rude."

"Sorry, Mother. I've had a difficult afternoon."

Eleanor nodded. "You threw him out, of course."

"I asked him to leave. He did, but only after making more vague threats about taking me to court for custody of Aubrey."

"We'll see about that! If he thinks he can just take that boy away from us, despite Jerome's wishes, then he is very, very wrong."

"Maybe we'd better talk about this later, Mother. I'm afraid Jon isn't getting a good first impression of our household."

"Jonathan is here to advise us on security," Eleanor reminded her. "Surely that includes taking measures against further harassment by Howard Worley."

"Has Worley been harassing you?" Jon asked, directing the question to Eleanor.

"He insists on visiting Aubrey at least twice a month," Eleanor answered irritably. "Aubrey doesn't care for him, and I'm positive Howard is no more fond of the boy, but he comes, anyway. We think he's hoping to find some reason to file a custody suit. He's very critical of the way Amanda and I are raising Aubrey."

"Critical in what way?"

Eleanor only made a disgruntled sound, and it was Amanda who reluctantly answered. "He's very snide about Aubrey's personality. He calls him a sissy and a bookworm—to his face! He criticizes Aubrey's parents, with whom he never got along, for the way they raised him before they died, and he accuses us of making bad matters worse."

"There is absolutely nothing wrong with the way Aubrey is being raised," Eleanor insisted. "Worley simply doesn't realize what a special child my grandson is. My son and his wife recognized Aubrey's gifts very early and encouraged him from infancy to develop to his full potential. They would want us to continue the curriculum they set for him."

Had Jon not been less perceptive, he might have thought Eleanor rather unfeeling when she spoke of her late son. As it was, he heard the hint of mourning in her steady voice, caught a glimpse of the sadness in her sharp blue eyes. Just as he'd noticed the way Amanda's soft mouth had trembled slightly when Aubrey's parents were mentioned. There was a lot of grief in this household, despite the stiff upper lips. He wondered if any of the family—Eleanor, Amanda or Aubrey—ever allowed that grief to surface.

As for the obnoxious Worley, was there any possibility that the kidnapping attempt had been a ploy to get his hands on Aubrey's money without going to court in what would probably be an unsuccessful custody suit?

"All right," he said, crossing his arms over his chest and making himself as comfortable as possible on the sofa he was coming to despise. "Tell me about the kidnapping attempt. From the beginning. If I have any questions, I'll break in with them."

BETWEEN AMANDA'S narration and Eleanor's frequent interruptions, it took Jon a while to feel satisfied that he'd heard everything they knew. He began to frown as the story unfolded and the extent of the would-be abductor's knowledge of the family became clear. It was beginning to sound as though Amanda and her mother weren't paranoid, after all. Someone had targeted Aubrey for a kidnapping, and Jon was no more confident than the boy's worried family that another attempt wouldn't be made.

"You said Terry was late picking the boy up because of a flat on the Lincoln?" he asked, looking at Amanda.

She nodded. "He didn't notice it until he opened the driver's door to get in. He said he changed it as quickly as he could, but it was almost four-twenty when he arrived at the library."

"The Lincoln was parked here?"

"No. At his mother's house, near the library," Amanda corrected. "Terrence almost always visits his mother while Aubrey studies at the library—or rather, he did in the past. From now on, he'll be staying with Aubrey if neither Mother nor I are free to go."

"So if the flat tire was no coincidence, we have to assume that whoever is behind this knew of Terrence's habit of visiting his mother on Wednesday afternoons."

"Or followed him to his mother's house, disabled the car while he was inside and then returned to the library for Aubrey," Amanda added.

Jon nodded to concede the equally plausible explanation. "Right. Terry had proof of the flat, I assume?" he asked, making the question sound as casual as he could.

Both Amanda and Eleanor stiffened. "Terrence has been in my employ for eight years, since he was nineteen," Eleanor said coolly. "My husband and I made it possible for him to finish high school and begin night classes at the university while supporting his wife and the child who was born just before he came to work for us. When my husband died two years ago, leaving me alone in this house, Terrence seemed to feel responsible for taking care of me. Even on his days off, he never fails to call and check or see if I need him to take me anywhere or run any errands. I won't have you questioning his loyalty to me or to Aubrey, is that clear?"

Realizing that Jon was startled by Eleanor's vehemence, Amanda interceded. "I understand why you'd ask, Jon, but you have to understand that Mother and I are very fond of Terrence. We were dismayed when the local police spent a long time grilling him about why he was late arriving at the library Wednesday. They treated him like an accomplice in the kidnapping attempt and seemed very suspicious of his story about what really happened, even though his mother and his sister both testified that he had, indeed, changed a tire before leaving for the library. He even produced the flat tire as evidence."

"Cops gave him a hard time, did they?" Jon's frown deepened as he pictured the smiling, easygoing young man who'd picked him up at the airport.

"Terrence got into some trouble as a teenager," Amanda admitted, choosing her words with care. "He hasn't been involved in any mischief for years, but the local police apparently have very long memories."

"I'm sure he appreciates your faith in him," Jon murmured.

"I can't imagine who would be behind this vicious plot, but I know it isn't Terrence," Eleanor pronounced flatly. "Howard Worley would be a more likely suspect."

"Now, Mother..."

Jon lifted a hand. "There were no other witnesses at the library? No one saw the woman drive away?"

"No," Amanda replied with a frustrated shake of her head. "There were very few people around that afternoon, and the woman was gone by the time Aubrey notified the librarian. Aubrey said something about bumping into a young woman with a baby as he was running away, but she wasn't located."

"That's not much to go on," Jon muttered.

"No. That's what I keep pointing out to Mother," Amanda agreed with a sidelong look at Eleanor.

"Have there been any other unusual occurrences? Any strange phone calls? Strangers hanging around the grounds or trying to talk to Aubrey?"

"No. Not that we can remember," Amanda replied. "The police have already asked these questions."

Jon nodded. "What about the gates at the entrance to your property? I noticed they were open when Terrence drove me in. Are they always left open during the daytime?"

"They're open all the time," Amanda admitted after a quick, somewhat sheepish look at her mother. "They haven't been closed in so long that the hinges have rusted open. We just never thought it was necessary to lock ourselves in here."

"They were always so much trouble to open and close all the time," Eleanor complained. "We stopped bothering with them thirty years ago."

"Then it's time to have them repaired," Jon said bluntly. "And you can have automatic openers installed on them that will operate from your car. The extra security is well worth the small inconvenience they'll cause you."

Eleanor sighed, but nodded. "We did ask for your advice."

"Right. Next step is a security system for the house."

"We have dead bolts on every door, and every window is locked," Amanda pointed out.

"Not enough. You need alarms and motion lights at the very least. Even if Aubrey is in no further danger, certain security precautions are a necessity these days. And how the hell did Worley just waltz through your front door earlier, anyway? Wasn't it even locked?"

He noticed that Amanda's hands tightened in her lap until the knuckles went white, and he suspected she was exerting a great deal of effort to keep from snapping back at him. But, dammit, did these people live in some sort of time warp? Didn't they know what a dangerous place the world had become during the past thirty years or so?

"I don't think I locked it after I let you in," Amanda admitted. "It won't happen again."

"Good."

"What are you going to do first, Jonathan?" Eleanor asked, looking at him in that confident too-positive way that reminded him uncomfortably of his mother. Jessie, too, thought Jon had all the answers, if only he'd bother to share them. He'd spent years trying in vain to convince her that there were some things he simply couldn't fix—even as a favor to her.

"I'll look around the place tomorrow, ask more questions about your routines and procedures. Then on Monday I'll start talking to some of the local security consultants about the most effective alarm systems for your estate. In the meantime, I want both of you to be thinking of everyone you know who might have even the most farfetched motive for having Aubrey kidnapped—everyone. Disgruntled relatives or employees, someone with an ax to grind against either of you, someone in serious financial straits. Your business interests are in banking, right?"

Eleanor nodded. "My husband's grandfather founded the Memphis Commercial Bank and Trust Company one hundred years ago. We are still major stockholders."

"Could be related to that. Someone who's been turned down for a loan or been foreclosed on—something like that."

"In which case, there could be dozens of suspects," Amanda said gloomily.

Jon nodded. "I'm afraid so. Our best bet now is to make sure no one has an opportunity to get to Aubrey again."

"I don't like thinking that my grandson has to be watched every moment," Eleanor said slowly, looking suddenly older. "It isn't fair to him."

"Yeah, well, no one ever promised that life was fair," Jon drawled, resisting the urge to point out that wealth had its disadvantages, as well as its privileges. He actually found himself feeling rather sorry for the woman.

It must be difficult for the daunting Eleanor Cummings Hightower to face her own vulnerabilities.

Eleanor delicately tossed her head and raised an imperious eyebrow. It was she who brought the conversation to an end, as though reminding him—perhaps even reminding herself—that she was still in charge of her life. "Has Amanda shown you your room yet, Jonathan?"

"Not yet, Mother. There hasn't been time."

"Why don't you show him around the house and then take him to his room? I'm sure he'd like to rest a while before dinner."

Jon had the distinct feeling that he'd just been ordered to his room for a nap. He looked at Amanda, who smiled back rather ruefully.

"I'd be happy to show him around, Mother, if he wants," she said.

Eleanor waved a hand, effectively dismissing Jon's wishes in the matter. "Fine," she said crisply, rising to her feet. "I'll be in the study making some calls if you need me. I'll see you at dinner, Jonathan."

Though he nodded politely, Jon wasn't particularly looking forward to a quiet formal dinner with Eleanor. To be honest, he'd rather have spent the evening hanging out on Beale Street with Terry.

As though she'd heard the thought, Amanda glanced back at Jon and made an apologetic face. "Mother doesn't mean to sound so officious," she explained. "It's just her way of phrasing things that sounds a little bossy sometimes."

He thought of his own mother's less forceful but just as inexorable methods of having her way. "That's okay. I have a mother of my own."

"Would you *like* a tour of the house?"

"Sure." He reached for his cane. "Lead on."

3

JON WASN'T AT ALL surprised to discover that the rest of
the large house was furnished as tastefully, expen-
sively and femininely as the front parlor. Trailing
Amanda through one room after another, he felt large
and awkward amidst the elegance. He couldn't help
wondering what she'd think of his one-bedroom, combination kitchen/dining room/living room apartment
in Seattle. Not that he didn't prefer his own place; he
did. He was comfortable there and his friends were
comfortable visiting.

He was as out of place here as, well, as Eleanor
Hightower would be at one of his pizza-and-TV-
football Saturday-afternoon gatherings. As for
Amanda—he looked at her sideways as he carefully
negotiated the flight of stairs leading up to the second
floor—he hadn't decided about her yet. She appeared
to fit nicely into this classy setting, seemed to be a
proper Southern lady all the way down to her Italian
leather pumps. Yet he couldn't help thinking that there
was another side to Amanda Hightower, and he
couldn't help wondering if she even acknowledged that
other side of herself.

Halfway up the stairs, Amanda noticed him wince
when he put too much weight on his right leg. "I

should have mentioned earlier there's an elevator you could use, Jonathan," she said.

He shook his head, annoyed that he was at a disadvantage in front of her. He didn't like how much she sounded like her mother when she used his full name. "Call me Jon," he reminded her. "And the leg will heal faster if I don't baby it."

She glanced down at his leg, then quickly back up at his face. "Were you injured on your job?" she asked.

He made a sound of self-disgust deep in his throat and wished he didn't have to answer honestly. If only he could claim he'd hurt himself rescuing a toddler from a speeding car or pulling an old lady out of a burning house or chasing a crook—or even getting some kid's cat out of a tree. Anything but the truth. "No. I, uh, fell off a bike," he admitted, not quite meeting her eyes as he reached the top of the stairs that led into a long, well-lighted hallway.

"Oh. A motorcycle." She didn't sound particularly surprised.

Damn. "No," he corrected reluctantly. "A ten-speed. I was, uh, sort of showing off for a . . . friend, and the damn thing got away from me on a hill. I was thrown into the side of a Dumpster and sliced my leg on a jagged piece of metal. Tore some muscle and some ligaments, but it should be back to normal in a few weeks."

Amanda didn't immediately respond. He glanced at her to judge her reaction, then found himself staring. Her brown eyes sparkled brilliantly, and she seemed to be fighting a smile. He'd thought her beautiful before; now he found himself literally forgetting to breathe as he watched her lower lip quiver and the small white teeth that sank into it to enforce control.

Misreading his expression, Amanda flushed. "I'm sorry," she said quickly. "I don't mean to laugh at your pain. It's just when I think that you were thrown into a Dumpster trying to impress a girl with your bicycle tricks, I . . . " She stopped when her quavering voice betrayed her amusement.

Jon forced himself to smile. "It's okay. I'm used to it by now. You should hear what my brother and sister and my friends have all been saying since I came out of surgery. I was expecting sympathy, and instead, I found myself the butt of everyone's dumb jokes."

Her eyes widened, humor vanishing. "You had to have surgery?"

"Just a few minor repairs," he answered, seeing no need to add that the woman he'd been with had been terrified that he'd bleed to death before the ambulance arrived. The doctors told him later that her fears had been unjustified. "Which way to my room?" he asked, deciding a change of subject was in order.

She motioned to the right. "My rooms are in the west wing on this floor. Aubrey's room and the guest room you'll be using are both in the east wing." She had told him earlier that her mother's master suite was on the ground floor.

Jon wondered how soon he'd have the chance to see Amanda's room. And under what circumstances. "Which door is mine?"

"First on the left. Aubrey's is directly across the hall. The two end rooms are unoccupied. Oh, and all the bedrooms have private baths, so you don't have to share a bath."

He nodded, trying not to look impressed. "What time's dinner?"

"Seven. And you needn't change unless you want to."

He'd bet his badge that the rest of the household always changed for dinner. At least he'd remembered to throw in some dress slacks and several good shirts when he'd packed. Right now he could use a hot shower, a couple of aspirin and an hour or so off his feet.

Amanda moved away, bringing the conversation to an end. "I have a few things to do before dinner. Is there anything else I can do for you now?"

"Oh, I could think of a few things I'd like you to do for me," he murmured, unable to resist baiting her a bit just to see how she'd react. "But they can wait until you get to know me better."

She blinked quickly, as though she wasn't sure she'd heard him correctly, then gave him a cool look that had to have been perfected through years of practice. If he was the fainthearted type, he'd probably have been unnerved. As it was, he was only amused. "I'll see you at dinner, Jonathan. Just call Roseanne if you need anything—there's an intercom panel in your room that will connect you with the kitchen."

"I'm generally pretty good at taking care of myself," he drawled.

She nodded. "I'm sure you are." With that, she turned and walked away, her back straight, her movements graceful and unhurried.

Jon strongly suspected that she would have stamped away in indignation if she hadn't known he was watching. So Ms. Hightower didn't care to be disconcerted, eh? Too bad. He was afraid he wasn't going to be able to resist doing so occasionally, he thought with a private grin.

As he turned toward the guest room she'd indicated, he noted that Aubrey's door was closed. Ordinarily he might have been concerned about rooming so close to a nine-year-old boy, but something told him he had nothing to worry about with this one. Young Aubrey was too well behaved to pester his grandmother's houseguest.

Damned strange household, he thought with a bemused shake of his head. He and his mother were definitely going to have a very long talk.

FRESHLY SHOWERED, shaved and dressed, Jon limped out of his room at ten minutes to seven. He'd spent a half hour or so psyching himself up for an awkward evening with sexy Amanda, her domineering mother and her odd little nephew. He was not looking forward to the next few hours.

He noticed the crack of light beneath Aubrey's closed door, and he paused, remembering Eleanor's admonishment to the boy not to be late for dinner again. Had Aubrey been in there for the past two hours, lost in his studies?

He knew it was none of his business, but with a shrug, Jon tapped on the door, anyway.

He heard a rustle of activity inside the room, and then the door opened. Aubrey was still wearing the shirt, slacks and tasseled loafers he'd had on earlier. His cheeks were slightly flushed and his glasses, perched on his snub nose, couldn't hide the look of guilt in his blue eyes. Had it been any other nine-year-old, Jon would have thought the boy had been up to some mischief.

He glanced idly around the unusually tidy bedroom visible through the open door, noting the open books spread on the crowded desk and the impressive computer system set up in one corner. Looked innocent enough. But Jon's job had trained him to search beyond the surface for clues. His deceptively casual observation came to a halt at the foot of the bed, where a black plastic rectangular box was just visible on the floor beneath the bedspread. Jon would have been willing to bet he was looking at one of those hand-held video-game systems, and that it had been shoved under the bed only moments before. Right after he'd knocked on the door, to be exact.

He stifled a grin. So, Aubrey Jerome Hightower wasn't quite as unnatural as he'd first appeared. Good. "It's almost time for dinner," he said casually. "I thought I'd ask if you wanted to walk down with me."

The boy's startled look and swift glance at his watch indicated he'd allowed the time to slip away from him. He checked quickly to make sure his shirt was neatly tucked in. "Yes, of course, Mr. Luck," he replied in his too-grown-up manner. "I'll show you the way to the dining room."

Jon didn't bother to tell him that he'd already been given a tour of the house. He knew all about saving face. After all, he'd once been a nine year old boy himself. Not as smart as this one, probably, but there had to be *some* similiarities. He was still trying to think of an opening gambit when they reached the top of the stairs.

"Would you rather use the elevator, Mr. Luck?" Aubrey asked, glancing quickly at the cane in Jon's right hand. "It's down at the other end of the hallway."

Jon shook his head. "I can make it. And call me Jon, okay? If you don't, I'm going to feel obligated to call you Mr. Hightower."

Aubrey chuckled, then looked almost surprised at the sound. Jon wondered how long it had been since the boy had laughed out loud.

Looked to him as if this household needed more than a security consultant. It needed to be shaken up, given an injection of fun and energy.

He reminded himself that he was there to give advice on protection, not on how the members of the household should be conducting their lives. *None of your business, Luck,* he told himself sternly. But he found his left hand rested companionably on Aubrey's thin shoulder as they walked side by side into the dining room.

Amanda sensed, rather than heard, Jon and Aubrey's arrival. She and her mother had just sat down, and the details of a charity event Eleanor had been describing were completely forgotten when Amanda looked up to find Jon watching her from the dining room doorway.

He'd changed into a white button-down shirt and dark blue dress slacks. His longish hair had been dampened and combed to lie neatly against his head, though it still brushed his collar in the back.

Amanda was rather surprised to see Jon's hand resting on Aubrey's shoulder and to realize that Aubrey wasn't shying away from Jon's touch. He wasn't a demonstrative child, having been raised by loving but decidedly reserved parents. Amanda hugged the boy occasionally and would have liked to do so more often but he always seemed so uncomfortable with the embraces that she held back. He didn't seem to mind at all, however, that Jon was touching him so casually. She couldn't help a tiny flicker of resentment.

"Oh, there you two are," Eleanor said, following her daughter's gaze. "Have a seat, please. Roseanne is waiting to serve dinner."

Still holding Amanda's eyes, Jon smiled, silently inviting her to share his amusement at her mother's officious tone. She returned the smile, though she quickly pulled her attention away.

Jon took the seat at her left and Aubrey slid into his customary place across the table. Amanda turned to make a polite comment to her guest just as he leaned over to lay his cane on the floor between their chairs. Their shoulders brushed and she drew back as though she'd come into contact with a hot object.

Even Jon's gaze felt warm as she pretended to concentrate on draping her snowy linen napkin across her lap.

"Aubrey, you will say grace this evening," Eleanor ordered as soon as everyone had been seated. To Amanda's relief, she seemed oblivious to the tension between her and Jon.

As always, Aubrey obeyed without protest, though Amanda thought she saw a fleeting flicker of discomfort cross his solemn young face. Bowing his sandy head, he drew a deep breath and murmured in a monotone, "For-the-nourishment-we-are-about-to-receive-by-your-grace-Father-we-thank-you-amen."

Jon made a sound that could have been a hastily suppressed chuckle. Amanda's lips twitched in response.

Eleanor lifted her head and gave her grandson a faint frown. "Thank you, Aubrey. Next time perhaps you'll put a little feeling into it."

"Yes, ma'am," Aubrey replied, reaching for his napkin.

Amanda looked up in gratitude when Roseanne entered with their salads. At least eating would keep everyone occupied for a few minutes. Assuming, of course, she could swallow with Jonathan Luck sitting so close to her side, his attention focused on her with an almost palpable intensity.

BY THE TIME the long stilted dinner was over, Jon had come to a few conclusions: Roseanne Wallace was one of the best cooks he'd ever encountered; the quiet formal Hightowers could definitely benefit from an injection of the Luck family's humor and energy; and the longer he sat so close to Amanda, the more his palms itched to touch her and find out if her glorious hair and flawless skin were as soft and appealing as they looked.

Get a grip, Luck. You're here to protect the kid, not to make a play for his aunt.

But then he and Amanda reached for the salt at the same moment, their hands touched, and he felt the impact all the way to his groin. So much for trying to remain detached. What the hell was it about this woman, anyway? She wasn't even his type.

Aubrey excused himself as soon as possible after dinner. With a touch of envy, Jon watched the boy leave the parlor, where Eleanor had guided them when they'd finished their meal. He wondered how soon he could make his own escape. His leg was throbbing with a vengeance, protesting the activity of the day, and the pain pills that would help him were sitting on the nightstand by his bed.

"You haven't mentioned your brother and sister since you arrived, Jonathan," Eleanor suddenly remarked, dashing his hopes that she would soon be ready to call it an evening. "How are Benjamin and Kristin?"

"They're fine. As I'm sure Mom's mentioned, Ben's an insurance investigator and Kris is an art teacher in a junior-high school. They both seem happy with what they're doing."

"Still no prospects of marriage for either of them?" Eleanor inquired.

Jon stifled a smile. "Not that I know of."

"Nor you, either, I suppose."

His grin broadened. "No."

Eleanor sighed and shook her head, glancing at Amanda as she spoke. "Jessie and I are beginning to wonder if our children will ever be settled with families of their own."

Amanda shifted uncomfortably in her seat and protested, "*Mother.*"

Eleanor launched into a monologue about when she and Jessie were young and how lamentably different the world had become. Jon and Amanda made the occasional contribution, but without a great deal of enthusiasm. Jon found his attention wandering more and more frequently, until finally he knew he had to make his escape or risk mortally offending his hostess by drowning her out with his snores.

He surged awkwardly to his feet and balanced himself on his cane. "If you'll excuse me, I think I'll turn in early. I'm a little tired from traveling all day."

"Is your leg bothering you?" Amanda asked, standing.

"Some," he admitted, understating the discomfort.

"Can I get you anything?"

"I have some painkillers in my room. But thanks."

"Be sure and let someone know if you need anything during the night, Jonathan," Eleanor said. He was surprised by the real concern in her voice.

"I will. Thanks. G'night."

His leg had stiffened even more than he'd realized as he'd sat there. Determined to maintain whatever dignity he could, he made his way carefully through the obstacle course of tables and breakables, horrified at the thought of crashing into anything in Eleanor's showplace of a home. When he was sure he was out of their sight he leaned heavily on his cane and his limp became more pronounced.

The leg was bothering him so much that he considered making use of the elevator, but he started up the stairs with grim determination. He wasn't going to get back to work until his leg was fully healed, he reminded himself. And he wanted to get back to work before his mother volunteered him for any more of these awkward "consulting" jobs!

A light showed under Aubrey's door. Jon heard a faint beeping coming from inside the bedroom and smiled. A video game, again. He wondered what Eleanor would say about that frivolous pastime. She certainly wouldn't hear about it from him, he thought as he let himself into his own room and headed straight for the painkillers on his nightstand.

AMANDA WATCHED Jon leave the room with concern for his obvious discomfort and a touch of envy that he'd been able to escape to the privacy of his room so early. She knew her mother would protest if she tried to do the same. Eleanor claimed to value these after-dinner visits, though Amanda often wondered whether her mother enjoyed them any more than she did or whether she was just clinging stubbornly to habit.

Once again, Amanda found herself thinking nostalgically of the years when she'd lived on her own, free to make impulsive, spur-of-the-moment plans, to kick off her shoes and sprawl on the couch with a diet soda and bowl of popcorn to watch TV—something Eleanor would never permit. Even after she and Edward had become engaged, she'd managed to cling to a couple of free evenings every week just for herself, to do whatever she wanted without worrying about consulting or offending anyone.

It had been wonderful. But that had been before she'd become responsible for a nine-year-old boy.

"Jon's an odd young man, isn't he?" Eleanor mused, breaking into Amanda's nostalgic reverie.

"I can't tell what he's thinking most of the time. There were even occasions during dinner when I wondered if he was laughing at us."

Amanda's lips twitched as she remembered the expressions in Jon's eyes a time or two during the evening, but she didn't hesitate to soothe her mother's concerns about their houseguest. "You've always said his mother has a rather quirky sense of humor. Perhaps Jon takes after her."

"I suppose so. Jessica does tend to find the most unexpected things amusing."

Not for the first time, Amanda wondered about the long-distance friendship between Eleanor and the school friend she'd seen so rarely during the many years since Jessica had married and opted out of the exclusive social circles that Eleanor cultivated so zealously. Amanda had always thought Jessica sounded very different from Eleanor and had marveled at the bond that had endured for so many years between the two women.

Eleanor sighed delicately. "I hope Jonathan knows what he's doing about our security. Jessie seemed so confident that he would take care of everything for us."

"I'm sure he's had a great deal of experience with security measures in his job with the Seattle Police Department," Amanda commented, not knowing what else to say to ease Eleanor's concerns.

"Homicide division," Eleanor murmured with a frown. "What a distasteful career. Yet Jessie says that Jonathan loves the job."

"He's probably drawn to the excitement."

"He does seem to be the adventurous sort, doesn't he?"

Amanda thought of his embarrassment when he'd told her about his bicycle accident and swallowed a laugh. "Yes. He does." She wondered if the woman he'd been showing off for on the bicycle had been more than a "friend." Not that it was any of her business, of course, she reminded herself sternly.

Eleanor sighed and shook her head. "Jessie's lucky, of course, that her children are all still living, despite Jonathan's reckless nature. It's so hard to outlive one's child. I don't know what I'd do if I didn't still have you, Amanda."

Hearing things like that from her mother always made Amanda feel as though someone had just set another hundred-pound weight on the already staggering burden she'd carried on her shoulders since the death of her brother.

She'd grown up rather spoiled and headstrong, rebelling against her mother's rules and her father's expectations. She'd been relieved that Jerome had been the ideal son to them, which took some of the pressure off her to conform to their wishes. After their father had died, Jerome had been there for Eleanor, leaving Amanda still free to pursue her own life. And then Jerome had died and Eleanor had been alone. And so had Aubrey, both of them looking to Amanda to take care of them.

It had been hard to walk away from the independent life she'd been living for so long, to give up the apartment she'd loved and move back into her mother's house with all the accompanying routines and requirements. But it had seemed the only logical step to take at the time.

And now it seemed that the only time she could be herself was when she was at the shop she hadn't been able to give up—or off on one of her mental trips to a tropical island. "If you'll excuse me, I think I'll go on up to my room now, Mother. I have a few letters to write this evening."

Eleanor nodded. "Perhaps you should look in on Jonathan when you go up. I didn't like the way he was favoring that leg when he left us. Jessie would want us to see that he takes care of himself."

Amanda swallowed hard at the thought of "looking in" on Jon, but she kept her voice bland when she responded. "Yes, I will. Good night, Mother."

"Good night, dear."

Wearily climbing the stairs, Amanda wondered if anything else could possibly go wrong today. Her houseguest had turned out to be more disconcerting than she could have imagined, and the first dinner he'd shared with them had been awkward and uncomfortable. Right now, Jon was probably wishing he'd stayed in Seattle—and Amanda wouldn't blame him.

No light shone from beneath his door and she wondered if he was already asleep. Her first impulse was to hurry off to the security of her own room, but she couldn't help remembering the way his mouth had tightened when he'd stood to leave the parlor. Though he'd tried valiantly to conceal it, he'd been in pain. She really should check on him.

She tapped lightly on his door, ready to slip quietly away if he didn't respond.

"Come in." His voice, muffled by the door, sounded gruff, but fully awake.

Feeling like an idiot for being so nervous and self-conscious, she turned the knob.

A toothbrush in his hand, Jon was standing propped against the doorway to his bathroom. He still wore the dress slacks and white shirt, though the shirt now hung untucked and unbuttoned. She kept her eyes on his face to avoid the sight of his appealingly tanned bare chest. He cocked his head curiously at the sight of her, then gave her a smile that all but seared her eyelashes.

"Did you stop by to tuck me in for the night?" he asked.

Lord, the man was impossible. Sympathy evaporating, Amanda lifted her chin. "I stopped by to check on you. Mother was concerned that your leg seemed to be bothering you. Is there anything I can do for you?"

She wished immediately that she'd worded the question differently. He gave her a devilish grin, set the toothbrush on the counter, turned out the bathroom light and limped toward her. "Oh, I'm sure I can think of something you could do to make me feel better," he murmured.

She frowned. "Do you always come on this strongly, Mr. Luck?" she asked coolly.

"Only when I find myself thoroughly intrigued," he said, stopping only inches from her.

Oh, he was good. And she was too tired to hold her own with him tonight. She backed quickly away. "One would assume you're too easily intrigued."

"One would be wrong," he replied, touching two fingers to her warm cheek. "I'm a little surprised by this myself."

She would have very much liked to ask him to explain what he meant by "this." She didn't, of course. Calling on one of her mother's tricks, she drew herself up and used a brisk no-nonsense tone when she said, "Well, then, if there's nothing else, I'll leave you for tonight. I'm sure you're tired—and so am I," she added.

"What you need," Jonathan suggested, taking another step toward her, "is a little relaxation therapy. Soft music, dim lights, a warm bath, a long slow back rub . . ."

Her head filled with images that made her knees go weak. "I think I'll settle for several hours of sleep," she said firmly. "Good night, Jonathan."

His smile held equal parts of resignation and challenge. This time he kept his distance. "G'night, Amanda."

She turned toward the door. She just wasn't up to this tonight. She really was tired. She hadn't slept well since the kidnapping attempt. Maybe after a good night's sleep, she'd be better equipped to deal with Jonathan Luck.

Maybe.

IT TOOK JON LONGER than usual to get to sleep that night. Maybe it was the way his leg throbbed from the day of traveling and activity. Maybe it was the strange surroundings—he'd never slept well out of his own bed. Or maybe it was the memory of how soft Amanda's skin had felt beneath his hand when he'd touched her cheek, or the way her eyes had widened and her lips had parted as he'd leaned close to her.

Calling himself a fool, he punched his pillow and settled more deeply into it. His mother would never forgive him if he made an ass of himself in her old friend's home. Though it went against his nature, he decided he'd be a perfect gentleman for the remainder of his visit—or at least until Amanda gave him some sign that she wanted him to behave any other way.

Yeah, right. In your dreams, Luck.

Trying to block out the mocking voice in his head, he buried his face in the pillow and at last fell asleep.

He didn't know how long he'd been sleeping when a scream brought him abruptly upright. A moment later he was on his feet, blistering the air with curses when his bad leg furiously protested the sudden force of his weight.

The scream came again and this time Jon realized the cries were coming from Aubrey. He didn't pause to grab his cane, but flung open his door, charged across the hall and burst into the boy's room.

The adrenaline rush was familiar, as was the reassuringly heavy feel of the weapon clutched in his right hand. Jon had slipped into the role of cop as easily and as naturally as some might have donned a bathrobe.

4

AUBREY WAS SITTING bolt upright in bed, trembling and staring at his bedroom window. "What is it?" Jon asked. The window was dark and he could see nothing to frighten the boy. "What's going on?"

"Someone was there," Aubrey answered in a small frightened voice. "In the window, looking at me."

Jon limped to the window. He stood to one side, looked through the open draperies. It was a clear cloudless September night and a full moon washed the grounds of the estate with a pale colorless light. Jon saw no hint of movement, no evidence that anyone was on the grounds. The full-length windows opened onto a small wrought-iron balcony, below which were bushes and hedges in a wide flower bed. Someone in good shape could probably climb over that balcony and look in the window. But why?

He turned back to the bed. "You can relax," he said reassuringly. "No one's out there."

"But there *was*," Aubrey insisted, still pale and shaking. "I saw him. He was looking in at me."

Despite his leg, Jon had been across the hall within seconds of the boy's crying out. Had there been time for someone to drop from the balcony and duck out of sight? He took a halting step toward the bed, keeping the gun unobtrusively at his side, wondering how to question the boy without upsetting him. "Could it have been a shadow passing over the window? A bad dream, maybe?"

"No!" Aubrey's wide eyes begged Jon to believe him. "There *was* a face. A pale scary face with dark hair all around. I saw it!"

"Aubrey?" Amanda rushed into the room, breathless and tousled and clutching a thick bathrobe to her throat. Her auburn hair tumbled around her shoulders, and her face, scrubbed clean of makeup, revealed a few faint scattered freckles Jon hadn't noticed earlier.

"Aubrey, what's wrong? What frightened you?" she asked worriedly. "Another nightmare?"

"There was someone at my window, looking at me," Aubrey said again. He was beginning to sound sullen, and Jon sensed that the boy was convinced no one would believe him.

"I'm going outside to look around," he said. "Amanda, you stay with Aubrey."

She looked at Jon for the first time, as though she'd been unaware of his presence until he'd spoken. She glanced at his bare chest above the black sweatpants, which were all he wore, then quickly looked away. Jon bit his lip to suppress a smile. Surely she'd seen a man without a shirt before.

"Shouldn't you put on some shoes?" she asked.

He ignored the question. "I'll be back in a few minutes. Aubrey, while I'm gone, you tell your aunt everything you saw, okay?"

Aubrey nodded. He looked very small and alone in his big rumpled bed. Leaving Amanda to comfort the boy, Jon left the room. He stopped by his own to step into a pair of loafers and to grab his cane, mentally cursing his need for it. He dug out a small flashlight he kept in his bag, then headed for the stairs.

He didn't really expect to find anything outside. He was convinced Aubrey had been dreaming—Amanda had said the boy had been having nightmares—but it wouldn't hurt to do something reassuring. Jon remembered what it was like to be a kid, how hard it had been at times to be taken seriously by adults.

The outside air was cool, the grass damp beneath his loafers. It was a quiet night, the sounds of city traffic muted and distant. Jon glanced toward the open gates of the estate and shook his head in exasperation. Anyone could have walked or driven through without difficulty. He was going to have to do something about that before he left.

He trained the flashlight on the ground beneath Aubrey's window. He saw no tracks, but then he hadn't really expected to in the lush, neatly clipped lawn. Already aching from the sprint across the hall, his knee strenuously protested the cool damp air. Muttering curses, Jon played the flashlight beam around the flower beds beneath the boy's window, convinced he'd find nothing out of the ordinary.

Something made him pause and look more closely at the large azalea bush directly beneath the balcony. He limped closer. The bush was squashed right in the center—as though a heavy weight had dropped into it from directly above. Jon bent closer and ran the flashlight beam over the branches. Recently broken, he realized as he looked at the fresh wood gleaming palely in the breaks.

Damn. Aubrey hadn't been dreaming. Someone *had* been on the balcony.

"What the hell is going on here?" Jon muttered, frowning up at the balcony above his head.

Amanda was still in Aubrey's room when Jon returned. Eleanor had joined them, her straight slim figure swathed in a heavy satin robe, her gray hair still immaculately styled. Aubrey, who sat in the same spot Jon had left him, looked distant and withdrawn.

Jon went straight to the boy and put a hand on the bowed sandy head. "Someone was out there," he said. "He's gone now, but he was there."

Aubrey looked up quickly, his eyes brightening with a combination of renewed fear and relief that someone believed him. "He's gone?"

"Yes. Amanda, call the police. Not that it'll do any good now, but we'll file a report."

"How do you know someone was there?" Eleanor demanded.

"There were signs. And besides, Aubrey saw him. Amanda, what are you waiting for? Call the cops."

She didn't like his autocratic tone and let him know with a glare as she left the room. Jon wasn't perturbed. What was with this household? he wondered in exasperation. Were they really as helpless as they'd acted since he'd arrived, or had he just caught them at a bad time?

"It's very late, Aubrey," Eleanor said. "Why don't you try to go back to sleep. We'll take care of the police report."

The boy glanced fearfully toward the window. Jon reached out and swept the heavy draperies closed, shutting out the night. "Might as well get some sleep, kid," he advised in a gentle growl. "After all this commotion, whoever it was is long gone. He won't be back tonight."

"You're sure?"

Jon ruffled the boy's already tousled sandy hair. "I'm sure. And I'll be right across the hall, okay?"

"Will you leave my door open?"

"You bet. Just give a yell if you need me."

"Is your gun loaded?" Aubrey asked curiously.

Eleanor stiffened. "Gun? What gun?"

The weapon was cool and heavy against the small of Jon's back, held there by the snug elastic waistband of his sweatpants. He left it there, knowing Eleanor couldn't see it from where she stood. "I'm licensed to carry," he reminded Eleanor. "Don't worry about it."

"I don't like having guns in this house, Jonathan. They're dangerous."

Jon didn't bother pointing out that whoever was after her grandson was more dangerous than the weapon he was fully trained to use. Eleanor just needed something to complain about, he told himself as he followed her to the door.

Amanda met them in the doorway. "An officer will be here soon to take a report," she told Jon. "They didn't seem particularly enthusiastic about it."

"I didn't expect them to be. Nothing really happened," he reminded her bluntly.

"Someone trespassed on our property," Eleanor argued heatedly. "I wouldn't call that nothing."

"The cops will," Jon returned with a matter-of-fact shrug.

Eleanor's look was scornful as she swept out of the room after bidding Aubrey a brief good-night.

Amanda hesitated at the foot of her nephew's bed. Jon waited in the doorway for her, watching, wondering if she would reach out to the boy now. Instead, she clasped her hands in front of her and asked, "Are you all right, Aubrey? Would you like me to stay with you until you go back to sleep?"

"No, thank you, Aunt Amanda. I'll be fine. Jon said no one would come back tonight."

Amanda glanced swiftly at Jon. He wondered if she resented the boy's confident acceptance of his reassurances. If so, she hid the emotion when she looked back at the boy. "Good night, then, dear. Call me if you need me, will you?"

Aubrey had already settled back into the pillows and pulled the covers to his chin. "G'night, Aunt Amanda," he murmured.

She hesitated a moment longer, looking uncertain, then turned and walked past Jon through the door. Jon looked after her in bewilderment. That was it? She wasn't even going to kiss the kid or anything?

He reached for the light switch. "G'night, kid," he said as he turned out the overhead light, leaving the room faintly illuminated by a night-light on one wall. "Give a yell if you need me," he said again.

"G'night, Jon. Thanks."

A doorbell chimed somewhere downstairs. Fast response from the cops, Jon mused, following Amanda down the hallway. One of the benefits of being an old-money family with heavy connections, he supposed. He quickly decided that those benefits didn't come close to making up for the look he'd seen in Aubrey's frightened young eyes.

As Jon had expected, the two officers who took the report didn't offer much encouragement that anything would be done. They gave the report a bit more attention after learning Jon's identity and hearing his evidence, but they agreed with him that there wasn't much to go on. Increasing the security of the estate seemed to be the only action to take at this point.

Jon saw the officers to the door while Amanda ushered her mother back to bed. He made sure all the doors were locked and the downstairs lights turned off after the police car drove away. Then he headed grimly for the stairs, frustrated with the family's lack of security consciousness. He muttered curses at the growing discomfort in his leg as he dragged himself up the stairs. Amanda was standing outside Aubrey's open door when Jon reached her. "He's asleep," she murmured.

"Good. I was afraid he'd be too upset to sleep."

"He was exhausted, I guess."

"Yeah." Jon knew he was being rather curt, but he was still thinking of the lost expression in Aubrey's eyes, how small and scared he'd looked in that big bed.

How Amanda, like her mother, had made no effort to offer maternal comfort. He remembered a few nightmares in his own childhood, remembered his mother holding him in her arms and soothing him. Kids needed that sort of thing—even kids with high-powered brains. And he found himself angry for Aubrey's sake that no one had offered it tonight.

Amanda Hightower baffled him as much as she attracted him. Her dark eyes could spark with temperamental fire or glaze with forbidding ice. One moment she was clashing with her mother, and the next she seemed to emulate the older woman. She'd appeared concerned about her nephew, yet she'd made no effort to reach out to him.

Just what was it with this family, anyway? he wondered for the dozenth time. And would he never understand them, no matter how long he stayed here?

Too tired to think about anything but rest, Jon turned away from Amanda toward his room. The abrupt movement caused his abused leg to buckle beneath him. He caught his balance at the last moment with the help of his cane.

Amanda's hands reaching out to steady him were soft against his bare chest. "Are you all right? Did you hurt your leg when you went outside?"

"I'm fine," he answered shortly, embarrassed at the display of weakness. "Just tired."

Her face was close to his as she looked up at him, her usually smooth brow creased with concern. "Are you in pain? Is there anything I can do?"

Damn, but she was beautiful. Even this close—*especially* this close—with no makeup to disguise her flawless skin or charming splatter of freckles. Jon felt himself weaken at the hint of warmth in her wide-set brown eyes. He lowered his head toward hers, tempted to steal just one quick kiss, just one exploratory taste—and then he caught a glimpse of Aubrey's open bedroom door from the corner of his eye.

Her nephew had needed her solicitous care more than he did. He didn't feel comfortable taking advantage of what the boy had been denied.

He stepped back with more haste than caution and suppressed a wince at the resulting twinge. "It's getting late. We both need some rest. Good night, Amanda."

Her hands fell to her sides. What might have been disappointment flashed briefly through her eyes—but then, he could have been mistaken. He really didn't know her at all.

"Good night, Jon. Thank you for your assistance this evening," she said formally. "I'm sorry your visit has been so chaotic."

"Yeah, well, that's why I'm here, isn't it?" he drawled, and turned toward his bedroom without waiting for a reply.

AMANDA WASN'T SURE what made her feel guiltier Monday morning—leaving for work or wanting so badly to do so. It felt good to drive away from her demanding mother, her withdrawn nephew and the thoroughly bewildering man who'd been volunteered to help them. And yet she felt as though she was cravenly running from her responsibilities, escaping from problems that had become more than she could handle. Maybe she was selfish, maybe she was a coward, but oh, it felt good to get out!

She'd called her shop Amanda's Emporium, simply because she'd liked the way it sounded. Quaint and old-fashioned, like the eclectic assortment of gifts and knickknacks she stocked.

She'd battled her parents from the day she'd opened the shop in a trendy Germantown shopping center. Her father had wanted her to go into banking, particularly after Jerome had declared himself too wrapped up in his intellectual pursuits to pursue such a practical mundane career. Eleanor still insisted on referring to the shop as "Amanda's little hobby." She seemed to think the hours Amanda devoted to her work would be better spent in the society charity organizations she valued so highly.

Even Amanda's friends, most of whom had careers of their own, wondered why she worked so hard when there were so many more interesting things to do when one had money. Oddly enough, only Edward, the sociology professor she'd met a couple of years earlier at a charity fund-raiser, had fully supported her in her business efforts, asking questions about her work and her plans, making suggestions that had come in surprisingly useful, though he'd had little business experience of his own. He'd encouraged and applauded her when few others had, and Amanda believed she'd slid into an engagement with him mostly out of gratitude. She was just glad she'd realized in time that a marriage should be founded on much deeper emotions than gratitude, emotions that simply hadn't been there between Edward and her.

Amanda was the first to arrive at the shop, but her assistant manager, Tricia Bowman, wasn't far behind. "Good morning," Tricia called out as she entered Amanda's small office at the back of the store. "How was your weekend?"

"Interesting," Amanda admitted, looking up from the paperwork on her desk. "Looks like business was pretty good Saturday."

The shop was closed on Sundays. Amanda usually worked Saturdays, but had taken the past one off to greet Jon. It was a great relief to her that she had someone she trusted implicitly to be in charge on the rare days she wasn't there. She didn't know how she'd manage without Tricia, who was punctual, conscientious, good with customers, and a whiz with numbers—something Amanda particularly admired, since she herself was lousy with them. Her frustrating inability to remember numbers—she was lucky to recall her own phone number!—had forced her to go to extreme measures at times to keep up with her studies when she was in college.

"Saturday was a good day," Tricia agreed, sounding pleased. "Had a rush on crystal items—lots of wedding showers coming up, I guess."

"Yes, well, it's that time of year. How did Kelly do?"

"I think she's going to work out just fine. You should see her go to work on the browsers. She has a knack of convincing them they really should buy something before the opportunity's gone."

"I hope she does work out. I'd hate to have to retrain anyone else soon. It's such an inconvenience."

"Mmm. So, what's going on at your house? Have the police come up with any leads on who tried to grab Aubrey last week?"

"No. And something else happened Saturday night." Glancing at her watch to make sure she still had several minutes before opening time, Amanda told Tricia about Aubrey's insistence that he'd seen a face in his window and Jon's belief that he'd found evidence to support Aubrey's claim. She and Tricia had been friends even longer than they'd been coworkers, so Amanda didn't feel awkward discussing personal business with her.

"I can't believe someone had the nerve to go right up to Aubrey's window!" Tricia exclaimed. Her permed blond waves bounced around her face in her agitation. "You must have been scared half to death."

"I might have been if Jon hadn't been there," Amanda admitted. "As awkward as it is at times, it was nice to have a police officer staying in the house with us when this happened. You should have seen how swiftly he responded to Aubrey's scream."

"So tell me about this Detective Luck. What's he like?"

"I don't know him well enough to answer that yet."

"Is he single?"

"Yes."

"Good-looking?"

Amanda remembered the way he'd looked wearing nothing but snug sweatpants, his dark hair tumbling around his face, his emerald eyes gleaming dangerously, his bare shoulders broad and tanned, his chest sleek and well developed. Her palms tingled, as though she was feeling that warm smooth skin again when he'd stumbled outside his bedroom.

They'd been standing very close together, his face so close to hers she'd felt his breath on her cheek. For a moment, she'd thought he was going to kiss her, and she wasn't at all sure she'd have resisted. But then his expression had suddenly hardened and he'd pulled back with an abruptness she hadn't understood.

Why had he suddenly changed his mind? Had his earlier flirting been nothing more than the habit of a man accustomed to being noticed and admired by women? He'd certainly kept a polite distance all day Sunday, which made her wonder if she'd only imagined the attraction she'd sensed he felt for her that first evening after he'd arrived.

"He's attractive enough in a rough sort of way, but I certainly don't have any personal interest in him, other than his expertise in keeping Aubrey safe," she fibbed.

"Hmph." Tricia eyed her friend and employer with open skepticism. "Well, if you're not interested, I sure wouldn't mind meeting him. Compared to the boring jerks I've been seeing lately, a handsome detective sounds delicious."

Flustered without quite knowing why, Amanda looked at her watch. "It's time to open. Want to unlock the front door while I finish going over this paper-work?"

"Chicken," Tricia taunted, though she turned good-naturedly to follow Amanda's request.

5

JON INSPECTED the Hightower house Sunday, looking for security weaknesses. Monday morning, he called some security consultants while Aubrey was in school, Eleanor out doing her volunteer work and Amanda at her shop. He made some notes outlining security recommendations for Amanda and Eleanor. After that, he drifted restlessly around the quiet, inhibitingly frilly house until Terrence brought Aubrey home from school.

Jon had rather hoped Terry would have some free time that afternoon, but Terry had a class to attend soon after dropping Aubrey off. "How about showing me around the grounds?" he asked Aubrey, eyeing the boy speculatively. "I've hardly been outside since I arrived Saturday."

Aubrey looked rather surprised that Jon had asked and didn't exhibit much enthusiasm, but with customary politeness, he nodded. "What would you like to see?"

"Surprise me," Jon suggested as they walked through a French door that led to the back lawn.

It was a gorgeous afternoon, much warmer than it would have been in Seattle. Jon undid another button on the short-sleeved sport shirt he wore with dark jeans. "Nice day, huh?"

"Yes, sir. Very nice," Aubrey agreed courteously.

Not exactly a promising start. "What do you like to do on days like today?" he asked, following Aubrey through a beautifully tended rose garden scattered invitingly with curvy white wrought-iron benches.

"I like sitting in the shade and watching birds," Aubrey answered seriously. "And sometimes I bring my books outside and sit on a bench by the creek while I study or practice my violin."

"Creek?"

"Yes. It runs across the back of the property under those trees," Aubrey explained, pointing. "It has minnows in it, and tadpoles."

Other than the studying part, that sounded more normal for a boy Aubrey's age. "You like to wade in the creek and catch minnows and tadpoles?"

Aubrey's eyes widened behind his glasses. He shook his head. "Oh, I don't wade in the creek. Grandmother says I can't risk walking around with wet feet. My health isn't very good," he added almost apologetically. "That's why I've never played many sports."

Jon eyed the small but healthy-looking boy with a skepticism he tried hard to conceal. He'd be willing to bet there was nothing wrong with the kid physically. Was his grandmother trying to turn him into a little neurotic?

Not for the first time, Jon wondered what the boy's father had been like. "What do you do for fun if you don't participate in sports? You like movies? Games?"

"I do like some movies," Aubrey replied. "Ones my grandmother thinks are suitable for my age, of course."

Jon almost shuddered at the thought of the films Eleanor would approve. "Games?"

"I'm in the chess club at school. I'm very good at it."

"I'm sure you are," Jon answered honestly. He paused to study a permanently installed but apparently little-used croquet court on the other side of the rose garden. When he spoke again, it was in a studiously casual tone. "What about video games? You like those?"

From the corner of his eye, he saw a guilty expression flicker across the boy's face. "Um ... Grandmother says video games are a frivolous waste of time. She says they encourage laziness and dull the mind."

Jon swallowed a word he was quite sure Eleanor wouldn't think fit for her grandson's ears. "I'm not saying your grandmother is wrong, of course, but I think a certain amount of fun and frivolity are necessary for a well-rounded personality. There's more to life than intellectual pursuits, you know."

Aubrey pursed his lips and cocked his head, obviously taken with Jon's argument.

Jon didn't push for confidences. Instead, he said, "Listen, you mind if I call you A.J.? Aubrey Jerome is quite a mouthful."

"A.J.?" the boy repeated in surprise. "A nickname?"

"Yeah."

"I've never had a nickname before."

Jon shrugged. "I can always call you Aubrey, if you'd prefer."

"No," the boy answered just a bit too quickly. He cleared his throat and tried to sound casual. "A.J.'s fine," he granted magnanimously, then frowned. "But I don't know if Grandmother will like it."

"That's okay. I'll just keep calling *her* Eleanor."

Aubrey giggled. Jon found the sound refreshing from this too-serious little boy. "I mean, I don't know if she'll like it if you call *me* A.J."

"Well, I guess that's between you and me, isn't it?"

Aubrey lifted his chin. "Yeah. I guess it is."

Jon was amused at the boy's unconscious imitation of him. "A.J. it is, then." He held out his right hand. Aubrey solemnly shook it.

"Aubrey? Aubrey, are you out here?"

At the sound of the voice both of them looked toward the house. "It's Aunt Amanda," Aubrey said, his face settling back into its usual lack of expression.

Jon tried not to scowl as he turned with the boy in the direction of Amanda's voice.

AMANDA SPOTTED Jon and Aubrey and headed toward them with a smile. Her smile faded and her steps faltered at the sight of Jon's face. He didn't look glad to see her; just the opposite, in fact.

If this continued, she thought wryly, she'd be tempted to believe her houseguest didn't like her very much. She wondered what she'd done to merit his displeasure. He'd seemed friendly enough at the beginning.

"You two out enjoying the lovely weather?" she asked, unable to think of anything else to say at the moment.

"I was showing Jon around," Aubrey explained.

She noticed how closely he was standing to the man, the admiration in his voice when he said Jon's name. She'd never known Aubrey to take to anyone so quickly. He certainly hadn't seemed to care for Edward. "That's very nice, Aubrey. Did you show him the spot by the creek where you like to practice your violin?"

"We haven't made it that far yet," Jon answered, resting a hand on Aubrey's shoulder. "We'll save the creek for next time."

Amanda glanced at his cane, noting that he was gripping it rather tightly. "How's your leg?"

"It's okay."

"Good." She pushed her hands into the deep pockets of her full floral skirt and tried to think of something else to say. Jon and Aubrey had seemed to be talking easily enough when she'd found them, she thought wistfully. Why was it so difficult for her to join in? "How was school, Aubrey?"

"I have a lot of homework."

"Oh. Then I suppose you'd better get started before dinner, shouldn't you?"

"Yes, ma'am." Aubrey looked up at Jon with a shy smile Amanda hardly recognized. "I'll show you the creek tomorrow, okay?"

"You bet. Thanks, A.J."

A.J.? Amanda blinked, but Aubrey only smiled more brightly. "See you at dinner, Jon," he said. When he turned back to his aunt, his smile faded noticeably. "Excuse me, Aunt Amanda."

She nodded, then watched disconsolately as he headed for the house without looking back.

Jon studied Amanda's expression closely. Every time he had himself almost convinced that she was a rather cold woman who simply didn't care about the boy, he caught a glimpse of something in her eyes that made him wonder. Maybe she just didn't know how to express her feelings, having been raised by the fiercely reserved Eleanor Hightower.

Still, it bothered him. If he ever had kids—and he'd always planned on doing so someday—he'd want to have them with a woman who could offer them all the love and security children needed.

Amanda turned to find him watching her. Clearing her throat, she made a vague gesture in the direction of Aubrey's retreating back. "He seems quite taken with you. What's your secret?"

"No secret. I just like kids."

"Oh."

"How about you?" Jon asked a bit too casually.

"What about me?"

"You like kids?"

She made a rueful face. "I haven't been around them much. I'm very fond of Aubrey, of course, but I don't think he feels the same way about me." This time he thought he saw real wistfulness mirrored in her eyes.

Feeling himself warming to her again—*careful, Luck!*—Jon gave her a reassuring smile. "I'm sure he feels the same. It hasn't been very long since he lost his folks. You have to expect it to take some time for a young boy to get over something like that."

"I suppose you're right," she said, but she didn't look at all convinced.

Jon didn't like the hint of melancholy in her voice. He'd rather have her smiling, or even spitting mad. He figured he could bring about either of those results if he set his mind to it. "Your hair looks beautiful in the sunlight," he said, admiring the way the late-afternoon sun brought out the red in the rich auburn tresses. "It must cost you a fortune to keep it that color."

To Jon's hidden satisfaction, her chin lifted and the sadness in her eyes vanished in a flash of temper. "I do *not* color my hair," she informed him. "This shade is completely natural."

"No kidding? And what about those big chocolate eyes of yours? Are they always that dark, or do you wear tinted contacts?"

"I don't wear contacts. And before you get even more personal, let me assure you that nature also provided the rest of me. What—"

"Nature was very generous," Jon murmured, eyeing the nicely curved figure enhanced by her close-fitting blouse and full flirty skirt.

"—makes you think you have the right to ask questions like that?" she continued, ignoring his flattering interruption.

"No right. Just curiosity."

"You don't think such personal remarks are rather rude?"

"If you thought I was being rude, why did you answer?" he asked logically.

She opened her mouth, then closed it again.

He smiled at her expression and lifted his left hand to brush his knuckles lightly across her cheek. Her skin was soft, heated by a light flush. Thoughts of fresh, sun-warmed peaches flashed through his mind, making him long for just one taste.

He leaned closer until his mouth hovered only inches above hers. "What's behind that beautiful face of yours, Amanda Hightower?" he murmured, his tone light, but the question serious. "What are you really like?"

Her eyes, so close to his that he could see the tiny specks of gold within the rich brown, became wary. "What do you mean? I'm exactly what I appear to be."

She'd stiffened as he'd moved closer, but she didn't step away. He wondered if she was as curious as he was. He hoped so. "Oh, no," he said, still speaking so quietly that she had to strain to hear. "I don't think you're what you appear to be at all. I think there are a lot of surprises hidden behind that proper Southern-lady exterior."

Her eyelids looked suddenly heavier. She moistened her lower lip with the tip of her tongue—not a deliberately seductive gesture, he decided, but a nervous one. "What makes you think they're nice surprises?" she asked in little more than a whisper.

"I didn't say they were," he pointed out, only half his attention on the conversation. "But I'd like to find out."

Gripping his cane in his right hand, he slid his left around her slender waist and gently pulled her forward. She didn't resist. Nor did she pull back when his lips brushed hers, lightly, testingly.

She tasted better than peaches, he thought as he brushed his mouth across hers again. Much better.

Such whimsical thoughts fled when she began to respond to the kisses. Moist and slightly parted, her lips clung softly to his. His left arm tightened around her to bring her closer. He was just about to toss the cane aside and kiss her exactly the way he'd been wanting to since he'd first seen her when they were interrupted by someone calling Amanda's name.

Amanda tore her mouth from beneath Jon's with a gasp. "That's Roseanne," she said in a voice he hardly recognized. "I have to answer."

"I know." *Damn*.

She avoided his eyes as she stepped away, hastily running a hand over her hair. Jon could have told her she still looked crisp and fresh and professional-looking—except for the high flush on her fair cheeks, the glazed, heavy-lidded look to her eyes and her damp mouth that was a deeper red than usual. She looked as though she'd just been thoroughly kissed, and smoothing her hair wasn't going to change that. He wisely kept his mouth shut.

Who'd have thought prim, proper, reserved Amanda Hightower could kiss like that? Now he couldn't wait to find out what other surprises were hidden behind that cautious facade.

He had to hurry as he followed her to the house. She didn't once look back to see if he was there. A week earlier, he wouldn't have been able to keep up. He took it as a measure of his recovery that he wasn't far behind her now.

Roseanne was waiting by the back door. She looked from Amanda to Jon speculatively, but said only, "You have a visitor, Amanda."

"Who is it?"

Jon noticed that Roseanne answered without much enthusiasm. "It's Dr. Miller. He's in the front parlor with your mother. And Mrs. Hightower asked you to join them, Mr. Luck. I'll be bringing appetizers in shortly."

"Dr. Miller?" Jon asked Amanda when Roseanne turned to go back inside.

"Dr. Edward Miller," she explained, looking no more pleased than Roseanne had. "A, uh, family friend."

He remembered the name now. Edward Miller. Amanda's former fiancé. The "brilliant university professor," in the words of the obnoxious Howard Worley.

"I'm looking forward to meeting this family friend," he said grimly.

Still avoiding his eyes, Amanda preceded him into the house.

A VISIT FROM EDWARD was absolutely the last thing Amanda needed today. Her mind still reeling from Jon's kisses, it was all she could do to greet Edward civilly.

"This is a surprise," she murmured, one eyebrow lifted in question at his unexpected visit.

Handsome, lazily charming Edward Miller greeted her with an affectionate kiss that would have brushed her mouth had she not turned her head to present her cheek, instead. His smile, the one that made him so popular with the young women in his sociology classes, didn't waver as he pulled back. "I thought I'd stop by on my way home from the university to check on you and Eleanor," he said. "And the boy, of course. How is he?"

"Aubrey is fine," Amanda replied, stressing her nephew's name. Amanda was fond of Edward on the whole. His laid-back attitude and impulsive nature were a refreshing change from her family's rigid routines and expectations, but at times he annoyed her a great deal. This was one of those times.

Seeing the way he was watching Jon, she wondered if he'd stopped by more to check out their houseguest than to check on her well-being. "Edward, this is Detective Jonathan Luck. Jon, Dr. Edward Miller."

Edward murmured a suitable greeting to which Jon responded with an unintelligible mutter. Their handshake was barely long enough to be courteous.

Eleanor invited the men to be seated—*ordered* them to be seated would be a more accurate description, Amanda thought—then suggested that Amanda serve drinks. Amanda had to admit that her mother was making an effort to be hospitable, considering that she disliked unannounced visits and had never cared much for Edward. Eleanor had always believed Edward was more attracted to the family money than to Amanda herself.

It was true that Edward had a fondness for nice things, and he had good taste. Amanda knew he couldn't live quite as extravagantly as he'd like to on his associate professor's pay, nor on the proceeds from the critically acclaimed but rather obscure nonfiction book he'd published the year before. But he'd never given her reason to believe his feelings for her were based on anything other than her own attributes, even if she'd found she couldn't fully return those feelings.

Edward and Jon were very polite during the brief visit, almost painfully so. Amanda could tell from the first that neither man cared much for the other. She wasn't surprised. They couldn't have been more unalike—the elegant intellectual sociology professor and the gruff utterly masculine cop.

Pleasantries exhausted, an awkward silence fell in the room. Eleanor made no effort to fill it, nor did Jon. Amanda couldn't think of anything else to say. She looked at Edward. He cleared his throat and glanced at his thin gold watch. "I see it's getting late. I'm sure Roseanne is waiting to serve your dinner. I'd better be going."

He paused a moment, but no one spoke, though Amanda had to bite her tongue to keep from blurting out the dinner invitation her deeply ingrained Southern manners demanded. Edward smiled and rose gracefully from his chair. "Well, then. I'm glad to see you looking so well, Eleanor. It was nice to meet you, Detective Luck."

"Yeah. You, too," Jon replied, reaching for his cane, ready to see the other man out.

"I'll walk you out, Edward," Amanda offered hastily, still feeling guilty that she hadn't invited him to dine with them. She simply hadn't wanted to spend the remainder of the evening struggling to compensate for her mother's coolness or Jon's silence.

"No need for that, dear," he assured her. "I know the way. You stay with your mother and your guest." He bent his head to kiss her, too quickly this time for her to avoid the brush of his lips against hers. "You still have my number. Call me if you need me," he said warmly, squeezing her hand before he left the room with the rather regal manner that had always seemed to come naturally to him.

Eleanor barely waited until Edward was out of earshot before harrumphing. "Still hoping for a chance at the family money, I see."

"Mother," Amanda protested, annoyed with Eleanor for bringing up her old suspicions in front of Jon. "That's not fair. He only wanted to see how we are."

"He could have called."

"You know how impulsive Edward is. He probably didn't plan to stop until he passed the house."

"Impulsive." Eleanor repeated the word witheringly. "If you ask me, that young man doesn't do anything without calculation. You mark my words, Amanda. He fully intends to renew your engagement. He has financial difficulties, and he's certainly not going to let your money slip through his fingers if he can help it."

"Mother, you're—"

"Is there any reason to believe the guy really is interested in the family money?" Jon asked suddenly, looking thoughtful.

"Of course not," Amanda snapped before Eleanor could speak. "Mother has accused every man I've ever dated of being a fortune hunter. She seems to find it impossible to believe that anyone could simply be interested in me."

"Eleanor, do you have any real evidence that Miller has financial difficulties?" Jon asked, ignoring Amanda's outburst.

"No," Eleanor admitted reluctantly. "But I've always suspected it."

Amanda realized suddenly why Jon was asking these questions. She stared at him in disbelief. "You surely aren't suggesting that Edward had anything to do with the kidnapping attempt."

He shrugged. "I told you, Amanda, everyone's a suspect. Miller would have the necessary inside knowledge of your family routines."

Amanda threw up her hands. "This is absurd. I can't believe we're even discussing this."

Eleanor sighed and shook her head. "I have to admit, I can't see Edward jeopardizing his future on such a risky business, Jonathan. He is well established at the university and gained some respect within academic circles with the book he published last year. Kidnapping Aubrey is such a wild dubious scheme—more Howard Worley's style than Edward's."

"It must be someone we aren't considering—a stranger," Amanda insisted. "As much as I dislike Howard, I can no more see him involved in this scheme than I can Edward."

"We aren't ruling out any possibilities for now," Jon said with a shrug.

"I'm going to check with Roseanne about dinner," Eleanor announced, heading for the door. "The two of you would probably like to wash up." As usual, her suggestion sounded very much like instructions to pre-schoolers. Amanda wondered if Jon was getting tired of Eleanor tossing out orders, though she could detect no sign of it on his face.

"Eleanor's right about one thing," he said when they were alone.

Amanda eyed him suspiciously. "What's that?"

"Miller does seem to expect you to fall right back into his arms."

Annoyed, she lifted her chin and headed for the doorway. "I," she said loftily, "don't fall into *any* man's arms."

His cane shot out just as she passed him, and she stumbled over it. Jon caught her as she pitched forward. "Don't you?" he murmured, his smile wicked.

She clung to his shoulders, but only to help her regain her balance, she assured herself. "You," she began, "are a—"

Whatever choice name she might have called him was lost when he crushed her mouth beneath his.

This, she realized, was the kiss she'd been waiting for in the rose garden. Deep. Hot. Delicious. Terrifying.

She didn't even try to resist it.

It was Jon who finally drew back. Jon who steadied her as he set her firmly aside. "I'll go wash up for dinner now," he muttered, leaving the room as quickly as his limp would allow.

Amanda was left staring after him, winded and bemused.

She shook her head and crossed her trembling hands at her waist. Just what was going on here, anyway? How had her dull predictable life suddenly gotten so complicated?

6

Wednesday morning, Jon made a long-distance call, charging it to his calling card. When a man's voice answered at the other end, he smiled and said, "Happy birthday, little brother."

"Hey, you remembered!" Ben sounded pleased. "Thanks."

"Everything going okay?"

"Okay here. How about you? Having fun doing another of Mom's little favors?"

Jon grimaced. "That is not funny, Benjamin. When are we going to learn how to say no to her?"

"Don't ask me. Every time I try, she gets that quivery-lipped, Bambi-eyed look and I crumble. Like the time she asked me to go into that biker bar to bring out the underage, rebellious son of one of her friends. Man, I was lucky to get out of that one with all my teeth! As it was, I had a black eye that didn't go away for days."

"I remember. Have you forgotten the time she wanted me to 'have a little talk' with those rotten kids who lived down the street? She said they'd respect me because I was a cop, and they'd stop terrorizing the neighborhood."

Ben snickered. "I remember. The oldest kid—what was he? eight? nine?—anyway, he kicked you right in the, um, zipper, and the little one bit a plug out of your hand."

"Right. Then the little monsters egged my Corvette. Then their father cussed me out when I told him he was going to have to do something with those budding criminals."

"And all because Mom needed a little favor."

"I know. Dammit, the woman's a master of manipulation."

"Too true. We're putty in her hands and she knows it. So, how's it going? Found any leads on the would-be kidnappers yet?"

"Ben, I'm here to set up a security system, not investigate the incident. I'm out of my jurisdiction, remember?"

"Right." Ben sounded unconvinced. "What have you learned?"

Jon shrugged. "Not much," he admitted, and briefly outlined the kidnapping attempt and the apparent break-in effort during his first night in the house. "I talked to one of the investigating officers this morning. The only suspect they've questioned so far is the boy's maternal uncle, and the questioning made the guy so irate he's threatening lawsuits against everyone involved. The problem is, we have no witnesses to either incident. No one except the boy, of course."

"Jon, you think there's a chance the boy is fantasizing this stuff? A bid for attention, maybe?"

Resisting his first impulse to deny the possibility, Jon took a moment to think objectively before answering. He pictured a lonely, intelligent, imaginative little boy, starving for attention from his aunt and grandmother, and had to admit that the question was a fair one. But then he remembered the look in Aubrey's eyes when he'd burst into the boy's room the night of the attempted break-in.

"No," he said, "he's not making it up. Something's going on. I just wish to hell I could figure out what."

"You think the kid could really be in danger, then?"

"Yeah," Jon replied reluctantly. "I think it's a definite possibility."

"Damn. Wish I could get away for a few days. I'd join you there, see if together we could come up with something. But I'm tied up with an investigation that's about to break wide open. It'll be weeks before I'll have any time off."

"Don't worry about it, Ben. I can handle this," Jon assured him, hoping he hadn't spoken too confidently.

"Just be careful, okay? We both know you tend to be a little, uh, reckless, at times."

"Reckless?" Jon repeated, twirling his cane. "Nah."

Ben chuckled. "Whatever. Just take care of yourself, big brother."

It'd felt good to touch base with his real life again, Jon thought, if only for a few minutes. Ever since he'd arrived in Memphis—or, more precisely, ever since Amanda Hightower had opened her door to him—he'd felt just a bit disoriented. Not quite like himself. And he wasn't sure exactly how to interpret his confusion.

IT HAD BEEN a quiet morning in Amanda's Emporium, giving Amanda and Tricia plenty of time to unpack a new shipment of Enesco figurines and arrange them in a freshly shined glass display case. Amanda had just set the last little bride on its shelf when the door banged shut. Someone, she thought with a slight frown, had entered rather roughly.

She looked over her shoulder and groaned at the sight of the mean-looking, shabbily dressed man who'd staggered in. Turning, she shared a quick rueful look with Tricia. "What do you want, McFarland?" she asked.

"I want the money you owe my woman," the man snarled, advancing toward her with a marked unsteadiness that indicated he'd been drinking.

"And I told you," Amanda said coolly, standing her ground as he neared her, "that I don't owe Nancy anything. She was caught stealing from the register. She's lucky I did nothing more than fire her."

"You're lying!" McFarland snapped, his dark eyes glinting with malice beneath a mass of greasy black hair. "You owe her and I'm here to collect. And maybe you'd better throw in a little extra to make up for calling her a thief."

"I'm not giving you any money, McFarland. Now either get out of my shop or we're calling the police. Tricia?"

Tricia held up the receiver to the telephone behind the sales counter. "Want me to start dialing?"

"That's up to Mr. McFarland," Amanda replied, looking hard at the inebriated man. "What's it going to be? Will you leave quietly?"

"Not without Nancy's money," he said, leaning one hand threateningly against a delicate case filled with expensive crystal. "You go ahead and call the police, bitch. And let's see how much of this fancy merchandise is in one piece by the time they get here."

The front door opened, and Amanda sincerely hoped no one would be hurt in what was shaping up to be a nasty scene. She heard the muted sounds of Tricia pressing buttons on the telephone and prayed the police would arrive before McFarland had trashed her store.

"You don't want trouble with the police, McFarland" she said. "If you'd just leave now, without—"

"Is there a problem here?"

Amanda recognized the low, rough voice. What was Jon doing here?

McFarland looked around to find the source of the question. "This ain't none of your business. Maybe you'd better come back some other time," he warned. The shelf of crystal shook when he stumbled against it as he turned.

Amanda caught her breath as a Waterford candy dish rattled ominously.

"I think you're the one who'd better leave," Jon said quietly, looking solid and tough and rather dangerous as he faced the younger man. "Now."

Drawing himself up to his full height—a good three inches taller than Jon, Amanda noted nervously—McFarland moved away from the case of crystal and advanced on the man who'd challenged him. "You planning to make me?"

Jon braced his feet, looking fully prepared for a confrontation. "Yeah, as a matter of fact, I am."

McFarland gave a snort of drunken amusement. "Well, take your best shot, cowboy," he drawled, then swung at Jon with a doubled fist.

Jon moved sideways without apparent haste and reached out to intercept McFarland's arm.

Amanda closed her eyes, certain that her shop was about to be destroyed around her. She just hoped Jon wouldn't be too badly hurt. His poor leg would never hold up to a fight—even if McFarland was drunker than a skunk.

There was a thud and a curse, then a moment of silence. Amanda opened her eyes and felt her jaw drop. McFarland was lying on the floor with his face in the carpet, while Jon knelt on top of him, one hand at the back of the man's neck. He had McFarland's left arm twisted upward at a sharp awkward angle, and each time McFarland struggled against the hold, Jon applied a little more pressure.

McFarland finally subsided, crying out in obvious pain. "Dammit, you're gonna' break my arm."

"If necessary," Jon agreed equably.

"Wow," Tricia breathed, stepping close to Amanda's side. "Who *is* that?"

Before Amanda could answer, two uniformed police officers arrived. Jon rose rather stiffly and turned over his captive. Amanda hurried anxiously to his side, but he brushed her off with a look that warned her not to dent his ego in front of the other men.

"Dammit, she owes me money!" McFarland shouted, beaten and infuriated as his hands were cuffed behind his back. "A man's gotta right to get his money."

"I don't owe you anything," Amanda repeated, relieved that her voice was reasonably steady. "You will never get any money from me, McFarland, so don't bother to show up here again."

"Bitch," McFarland snarled as he was escorted outside. "You're going to be sorry about this. You'll wish you hadn't..."

The door closed behind him before he could complete his threats. Amanda sagged in relief against the counter.

"Are you all right?" Jon asked, moving toward her, his limp very noticeable.

"I'm fine. Are *you* all right?"

"Yeah. Guy was so drunk he could hardly stay on his feet. Who the hell is he, Amanda?"

"His name is Grady McFarland. I had to fire his girlfriend a few weeks ago, and he's been giving us trouble ever since."

One of the officers who'd escorted McFarland from the shop returned to fill out a report. Amanda assured him that she would be pressing charges and be happy to cooperate with his questions. Less than twenty minutes later, both officers and McFarland were gone—to Amanda's relief.

"I just have to meet this man," Tricia said, coming forward with a curious smile for Jon. "Who's the hero, Amanda?"

Rather amused to see the color mount in Jon's cheeks at the term "hero," Amanda made the introductions. "Tricia Bowman, this is Detective Jon Luck of the Seattle Police Department."

"So you're Amanda's detective. Her description didn't do you justice."

Jon grinned at Tricia's blatant flirtation. "Now why am I not surprised to hear that?"

For the first time since he'd entered the shop, Jon looked at the displays of fragile merchandise around him. Merchandise that was miraculously undamaged, Amanda thought gratefully, deciding she owed Jon a big favor.

"Nice place," he said.

"Thank you. What are you doing here, Jon?" Amanda asked. A sudden possibility occurred to her and she gasped. "Is something wrong? Has something else happened—"

"Aubrey's fine," Jon assured her, lifting a hand to silence her. "Nothing's happened. I just stopped by to see if I could take you to lunch. You haven't eaten yet, have you?"

"Lunch?" Amanda repeated blankly. She found it rather difficult to switch gears so easily from high drama to mundane concerns like food.

"She hasn't eaten," Tricia announced. "And she'd be delighted to have lunch with you, wouldn't you, Amanda?"

Amanda gave Tricia a warning look. "Well, I—"

"Great. I have some things I want to talk over with you," Jon said, considering the matter settled.

"But—"

"Don't worry about it, Amanda. I can handle everything here. It's not as if we're crawling with customers today," Tricia said wryly, waving an expressive hand around the empty shop. "And Kelly will be in soon to help unpack that new stock. Take your time."

Amanda sighed and gave up. After all, having lunch with Jon was the least she could do after he'd prevented McFarland from wrecking her place. She'd even pick up the tab, she decided magnanimously. "All right. I'll go."

Jon gave her a mocking nod of his head. "Thanks so much."

She resisted the impulse to glare at him, then suddenly frowned. "Where's your cane?"

"Left it back at the house. I was starting to get real tired of carrying it around—even though it has its uses at times."

His grin told her was referring to the incident before dinner Monday evening, when he'd tripped her with the cane and kissed her until her ears buzzed. She'd been trying very hard not to think of that kiss ever since—without much success.

"Are you sure you should be walking around without it?" she asked doggedly, avoiding his eyes. "Is your leg strong enough to support you without it?"

"Getting stronger all the time," he assured her. "But thanks for asking." With that, it was obvious he considered the subject closed. Male ego, she reminded herself belatedly.

Amanda had assumed Terrence had driven Jon to her shop. She was startled to discover he'd taken a cab. "Terry was tied up with errands for your mother this morning," he explained when she protested. "I didn't want to bother him."

"Well, you can't take cabs all over Memphis every time you want to leave the house. Can you drive?"

His eyebrow lifted as he buckled the seat belt in the passenger seat of her Oldsmobile. "Of course I drive."

"I meant can you drive *now*—with your leg," she explained, starting the car.

"Oh. Yeah. I can drive."

"Then I'll give you the keys to the Cadillac. You can use it when you want to leave the house."

"The Cadillac?"

"It was Jerome's car," she explained, swallowing a sudden lump in her throat. "Mother and I haven't gotten around to selling it yet. It's just sitting in the garage—you might as well use it while you're here."

"That would come in handy. Thanks."

The restaurant she selected was only a few blocks from her store. Normally she would have walked, but she hadn't wanted to put that much strain on Jon's injured leg, especially after he'd already overused it in the scuffle with McFarland. She chose a parking space and climbed out of her car, intensely aware of him at her side as they entered the trendy restaurant with its upscale lunch crowd.

Jon barely gave her time to be seated and place her order before questioning her more about the incident in the shop.

"Tell me more about that creep," he demanded, from across the small secluded corner table. "What other trouble has he caused you?"

Amanda shook her head. "It hasn't been that bad until now. He's made a nuisance of himself a few times, demanding that I reinstate Nancy or give them money and making wild threats about what he'd do if I didn't."

"Why did you fire the girlfriend?"

"She was stealing from the register. It took me a while to realize it, I'm afraid. I tend to believe the best of my employees, and I hated having to admit a woman I rather liked was stealing from me. But when I confronted her with the evidence, she admitted it."

"Are you prosecuting?"

"No." She took a sip of her water.

Jon frowned. "No? Why the hell not?"

"I just didn't choose to," she informed him coolly, seeing no need to defend her decisions.

Jon didn't appear to agree. He crossed his arms over his chest and glared at her. "You don't think she deserves it? And what about her next employer? You won't feel at all responsible when she rips him off, too?"

Amanda hadn't thought of it in quite that way. "I felt sorry for her," she admitted. "She's rather sweet, but terribly insecure. Very low self-esteem, which McFarland makes no effort to remedy. He treats her horribly—I suspect he even physically abuses her—but she adores him. She does whatever he asks without question."

"And you think he asked her to steal from you."

"I'm sure of it. Nancy would never have thought of it herself."

"You'd probably be doing her a favor to prosecute. Maybe she'd get away from the bastard."

"More likely she'd take the punishment for his idea while he got off scot-free," Amanda argued. "I didn't want to take that chance. I offered to help her if she wanted to leave him, but she got very defensive about him. Refused any help from me."

"What sort of threats has he made?"

"Nothing specific. The old 'You'll be sorry' clichés. I didn't take him very seriously."

"Maybe you should have. And you should have reported him to the police before today. Terroristic threatening is a crime in itself, you know."

"You seem to be telling me a great many things that I should have done," Amanda pointed out with a touch of resentment. "I made the decision to let it go, Jon. I really don't think I have to defend my decisions to you." Even though she had been doing just that, she thought in exasperation.

He shrugged. "Whatever. I just think it was a dumb decision."

"Well, I can't see that it's really any of your business," she grumbled. Her gratitude for his assistance that afternoon was rapidly wearing off!

He lifted an eyebrow. "Maybe it is my business. How do you know McFarland and his girlfriend weren't the ones who tried to grab A.J.?"

Amanda stared at him. "Surely you don't believe that."

"What does Nancy look like? Is she a chubby blond?"

"No, her hair is a mousy brown. Jon, this is—"

"But is she chubby? With a blond wig, could she have been the woman who approached Aubrey at the library?"

"Nancy is five feet two inches tall and weighs maybe a hundred pounds. She couldn't possibly be the same woman. Anyway, it's absurd. Nancy would do just about anything for that jerk, but I can't believe she would deliberately harm a child."

"Maybe he promised her the boy wouldn't be hurt. Maybe he's got her convinced that this is the only way for her to get the money he's so sure you owe them."

Amanda shook her head. "No. It couldn't be them."

Jon snorted impatiently. "So far you've firmly assured me it couldn't be Worley, Miller or McFarland. But *someone* tried to kidnap your nephew, Amanda, and we aren't going to find out who it was until you open your mind to the possibilities."

Amanda picked up her fork and stabbed angrily at her salad. She was seething at his arrogance, even though she had to admit he had a point.

It was a few minutes before Jon spoke again. When he did, he completely changed the subject. "I talked to my brother this morning. He's an insurance investigator back in Seattle."

Amanda looked back up at him with interest. "Were you consulting him about Aubrey?"

"Actually I was calling to wish him happy birthday. He's thirty-one today. But we did talk about what's been going on here."

"Did he have any suggestions?"

"One." Jon seemed to watch her closely as he elaborated, "He wanted to know if there's any possibility the kid's been imagining these incidents. Deliberately making them up, maybe."

Amanda huffed. "I hope you set him straight about that."

"I told him I thought the incidents had really happened. But I gave the matter some consideration first. It was a reasonable suggestion."

"Reasonable?" she repeated incredulously. "It's ridiculous! Why in the world would Aubrey make something like this up?"

"For attention."

Amanda firmly shook her head. "That's absurd. Aubrey is hardly hungry for attention."

"Isn't he?" Jon asked, his voice a bit too quiet.

"Of course not!" she answered, offended at the implication. "Mother and I are there whenever Aubrey needs us. We've tried to give him everything he needs since his—while he's lived with us."

"Materially, yes, the kid has everything. Emotionally. . . I'm not so sure."

Amanda stared blindly at the salad that had suddenly lost its appeal. "You think I haven't tried to reach out to him? I have. He won't let me. I don't . . . I don't think he likes me much."

Jon's voice became gentle. "Do you like *him*?"

"Like him?" she repeated, staring at him. "Jon, I love him. He's my nephew."

"Yes, but do you *like* him?" he insisted. "Do you really even know him? The things he likes to do, his feelings about losing his parents, his hopes and plans for the future?"

Her eyes pricked with tears and she blinked, determined to keep them dry. "How can I learn those things about him when he won't share them with me? I ask him questions and he answers in monosyllables. I try to encourage him to talk about his parents, and he completely withdraws. I ask what he'd like to do and he says he needs to study. He won't let me near him, Jon—neither emotionally or physically. Sometimes . . ."

Her voice broke. His hand covered hers on the table, big and warm and supportive. The tears she'd been trying to hold back flooded her eyes as she whispered, "Sometimes I want to hold him so badly, just take him in my arms and give him a big hug. But every time I try, he stiffens up. He doesn't like me, Jon. And I don't know what to do to change that."

Jon's fingers tightened around hers. "Amanda, I know you've tried hard to be a good guardian to the boy—too hard, perhaps. Maybe you should just relax, treat him like a normal little boy as much as possible, while still helping him develop to his full potential."

She couldn't help resenting his giving her more un-asked-for advice, even though she found herself hanging on every word of that advice. "What makes you such an expert on child prodigies?"

He gave a short laugh. "I'm not. Lord knows I wasn't one myself, but I *was* once a nine-year-old boy. I think Aubrey's lonely, and I think he needs to have some fun in his life. I'm sure if you'll relax and start treating him like a little boy, instead of a little genius, you'll find out he likes you more than you think."

Amanda bit her lower lip. "I don't know how much fun he can have as long as someone's trying to hurt him."

Jon's fingers squeezed hers once more and then he drew back, his face hard and determined. "I'll take care of that."

"I just hope you can."

"Trust me, Amanda. No one's going to hurt that kid while I'm around."

"The problem is," she pointed out reluctantly, "that you're only going to be around for a few more days. What happens after that?"

"I'll take care of it," he repeated.

Amanda turned her attention back to her lunch, though the thought of Jon's leaving had made what little appetite she'd had disappear. Did she want Jon to stay for Aubrey's sake—or was there more to it than that? She couldn't help wondering.

7

JON WAS WAITING at the foot of the steps, leaning against one of the marble columns in front of the house when Terrence drove Aubrey home from school that afternoon. He greeted the boy and the driver with a smile.

Aubrey tumbled out of the Lincoln with more haste than grace. During the past few days, Jon had sought the boy out on several occasions, in order to spend some time with him. By now Aubrey was very much at ease with him, as evidenced by his eager greeting, "Hi, Jon!"

"Hi, A.J. How was school?"

"Okay. Where's your cane?"

"I've retired it. Go put your things away and come on back outside, okay? Thought we'd go sit by the creek awhile this afternoon."

Aubrey pushed his glasses higher on his nose and smiled shyly. "I'll be right back."

"Stop by the kitchen on your way back out. Ask Roseanne if she has got some cookies or something we can take with us. I'm sure you're ready for a snack. We'll have one by the creek."

Aubrey looked over his shoulder. "Like a picnic?"

Jon grinned. "Yeah. A junk-food picnic. Be sure and tell Roseanne we don't want any healthy stuff—just good junk." Since he'd already made arrangements with the delighted housekeeper, Jon knew she'd have snacks ready.

Looking just a bit bemused, Aubrey nodded and hurried inside, his books clutched beneath one skinny arm.

Jon chuckled at the boy's uncharacteristic rush.

Terrence was looking after Aubrey with a look of astonishment. "What's *your* magic?" he asked Jon.

"What do you mean?"

"I've never seen that boy so animated. He really likes you."

"He's a good kid."

"He's always been polite enough, but he's never said more than a few words to me."

"Problem is he's shy," Jon explained. "He doesn't seem to know how to initiate conversation. He just politely responds."

"Guess that's what he's been taught. His parents were kind of . . . uh . . ." Terrence didn't finish, apparently concerned he was being indiscreet about his employers.

Jon had no such qualms. "What *were* his parents like?"

"Like his grandmother," was the careful answer. "Both of them. Nice enough, but kind of . . ."

"Rigid? Formal? Cool?" Jon supplied when Terry stopped to fumble for a word.

Terrence nodded. "All of the above."

The old children-should-be-seen-but-not-heard school, Jon thought grimly. "The kid needs to cut loose some. He needs to get dirty. He needs friends," he mused aloud.

The chauffeur nodded again. "That's what I've always thought, but I never knew how to suggest it. As a matter of fact, I've thought of introducing him to my own boy, though I don't know whether Mrs. Hightower would approve."

"Why wouldn't she? How old is your boy?"

"Nathan's a couple of months younger than Aubrey. Lot different, though. Nathan's an average fourth grader—his grades are okay, but he's no genius. He likes sports and TV and video games and stuff like that. I don't know how well he and Aubrey would get along."

"Maybe we should give it a try one afternoon after school," Jon said, thinking of the video game under Aubrey's bed. "They might have more in common than you think. And we'll tell his grandmother it was all my idea if she says anything."

"We'll do it, then." Terrence grinned and opened the car door. "I've gotta go. I'm free tomorrow evening, though. Want to go check out Beale Street with me?"

"You bet I do." Jon knew his eagerness to get out of yet another formal family dinner was apparent in his swift answer.

The chauffeur chuckled. "I'll pick you up at eight, then. Show you *my* side of Memphis."

"I'll be looking forward to it."

Carrying a brown paper bag in one hand, Aubrey reappeared just as Terrence drove away. "Mrs. Wallace had our snacks ready," he explained. "She said you'd already talked to her about it."

"Yeah." Jon pushed himself away from the post, determined to ignore the protest of his overused injured leg. "Let's go find that creek."

Roseanne had packed the bag with chilled canned soft drinks, brownies and apples. The brownies disappeared in record time and Jon and Aubrey solemnly agreed to forgive her for sneaking in the healthy fruit.

Jon had shed his shoes and socks to enjoy the feel of the warm grass under his feet. He'd had some difficulty convincing Aubrey to do the same. Only when Jon had assured the boy that junk-food picnics had to be eaten barefoot to be really cool had Aubrey slipped out of his trim loafers, tucking his socks neatly inside.

"You got any good friends at school?" Jon asked casually as they lounged in the autumn-browning grass, munching the apples.

"Not really," the boy admitted, plucking at the stem of his apple to avoid Jon's eyes. "They're all a lot older than me. Sometimes some of them make fun of me."

"How come?"

"Well, because I'm so small and wear glasses and loafers, instead of sneakers. And sometimes they call me—" he swallowed hard "—Audrey."

Jon scowled. "You just tell 'em to call you A.J. No one can say that's not a cool name."

Aubrey looked up bashfully. "I, uh, told one guy today he could call me A.J. He did. I kind of like it."

"Do you wish you'd stayed in fourth grade with the other kids your age?"

"No. Not really. I'd be really bored in my classes. But sometimes I wish . . ."

"You had more friends?" Jon supplied gently.

Aubrey nodded.

"Did you know Terry, uh, Terrence has a boy your age? His name's Nathan."

"Yes, he's mentioned him."

"Well, how'd you like the four of us to get together one afternoon after school while I'm here and go do some guy stuff? Check out the park or a ball game or something?"

Aubrey looked hesitant. "I don't know . . ."

"It'll be fun. You like Terrence, right?"

"He's very nice."

"And you like me, don't you?"

Aubrey's shy smile made Jon's chest tighten. "Yes."

"You'll probably like Nathan, too. How about it? Want to give it a try?"

"All right."

Jon ruffled the boy's hair. "That's the ticket. Now where are those tadpoles you told me about?" he asked, turning toward the picturesque tree-shaded stream running along the back border of the Hightower estate.

"Oh, there aren't any tadpoles in the fall," Aubrey said quickly, jumping to his feet. "Tadpoles are out in the spring. They're all frogs now."

"Well, darn," Jon complained, as though he hadn't been perfectly aware of that scientific fact. "Maybe we can spot some minnows."

Hands braced on his knees, Aubrey leaned out over the water and pointed. "See by that rock? There's a whole school of them."

"No kidding?" Jon stepped up behind the boy and obligingly looked toward the rock. "I don't see any minnows. Just a shadow."

"No, they're minnows," Aubrey argued earnestly. "See the way they move around the rock?"

"Optical illusion."

"Minnows," Aubrey insisted.

"Maybe you'd better look closer," Jon suggested, planting a hand on the boy's back and giving a slight push.

Aubrey stumbled, tried to catch himself, then landed calf-deep in the clear cool stream. He looked down at his wet trouser legs, then back up at Jon, his expression the picture of astonishment. "You pushed me in!"

Jon grinned. "Yeah, I did. What are you going to do about it?"

Aubrey blinked behind his glasses. "I don't know."

Fists planted on his hips, Jon sighed loudly and shook his head. "What's wrong with you, boy? Someone pushes you in a creek, you retaliate. Where's your spirit of revenge?"

For the first time in the few days that Jon had known the child, he saw a genuine spark of mischief light the usually serious young eyes. Quickly, Aubrey bent over, hands cupped, and scooped water in Jon's direction. The spray splattered Jon's shirt and jeans.

"Get me wet, will you?" Jon growled, delighted with the boy's response, and pushed the thought of Eleanor's inevitable disapproval to the back of his mind. "I'll show you, brat."

With that, he stepped into the creek, treading carefully on the rock bottom as he lunged playfully for the boy.

Aubrey squealed and evaded him, then splashed more water in Jon's direction. Laughing, Jon retaliated.

It was about time someone taught this kid how to play, he thought. Even if that someone had to be a near stranger who was only in town for a few more days.

AMANDA STROLLED through the backyard heading for the creek, where Roseanne had told her Jon and Aubrey could be found. She'd spent all afternoon thinking of what Jon had said at lunch, wondering if he could possibly be right that Aubrey wanted as badly as she did to get past the emotional wall between them. Wondering if she'd given the boy any reason to believe she didn't want to be closer to him. If so, it hadn't been intentional. She could only blame her lack of experience with children. But she felt guilty that she hadn't tried just a little harder.

The creek was still hidden from her view by the massive oak and pecan trees at the back of the property when she heard sounds of laughter. Jon's—and Aubrey's? She couldn't remember ever hearing her nephew laugh like that. Another noise that sounded like vigorously splashing water made her frown curiously and hasten her steps toward the creek. What in the world...?

She could never have imagined the scene that met her eyes when she stepped around a tree and stood beside the creek. Two dripping males gazed back at her, the smaller one looking sheepishly guilty, the larger one daring her with his eyes to say one word of criticism. She couldn't think of anything to say except, "Um . . . how's the water?"

"Come in and find out for yourself," Jon challenged her.

"I don't think so."

He grinned and headed toward her. She took two steps back in response to the look in his eyes. "Oh, no," she said warningly. "Don't even think about it."

Aubrey covered his mouth with his hands and giggled. The sound was so touching, so welcome that Amanda was tempted to let Jon dunk her, just so she could hear Aubrey laugh again. But . . . "This is a silk dress," she fretted, looking down at her favorite blue shirtwaist.

Jon stopped with an exaggerated sigh. "In that case, I'll let you off the hook. But if I ever catch you down here in jeans, you're going to get wet."

"I'll take that as a warning," she assured him. "Aubrey, you'd better go in and get cleaned up now. Your grandmother will be home from her Ladies' League meeting soon."

To her regret, Aubrey's smile immediately disappeared and his eyes became serious behind his water-splattered glasses.

Amanda was just about to reassure him that he wouldn't be reprimanded, when Jon spoke. "Don't worry if your grandmother kicks up a fuss, A.J. We'll tell her that my poor injured leg gave way, making me fall into the creek, and you bravely risked your life to save me. She'll think you're a hero. Probably give you a medal or something."

"If we go now, we won't have to tell her anything at all," Amanda added. "She's not due home for another half hour or so."

Aubrey promptly climbed out of the creek and snatched up his shoes and socks.

Jon followed more slowly. He winced when he stepped out of the water and placed his full weight on his bad leg. Amanda made an instinctive move toward him, but he held her off with a slight shake of his head. "I'm okay," he assured her gruffly. "Just overdid it a little."

"You, uh, want to tell me why you were playing in the creek?" Amanda asked politely, staying close by just in case his leg buckled. She bent to pick up his shoes and handed them to him with a casual gesture that belied her concern for him.

"Because it was there," Jon replied with an expansive motion of his free arm. "Jonathan Luck sees a challenge, he tackles it. No mountain too high, no stream too deep, no—"

"No way do I believe all this," Amanda interrupted to Aubrey's amusement. She saw the satisfaction and the approval in Jon's eyes when the boy laughed again, and she warmed at the realization that Jon was pleased with her for the way she'd reacted to finding them in the creek. And she didn't really have to ask why Jon had been cavorting in the water; Aubrey's rare laughter said it all.

They almost made it. They'd just reached the kitchen door when it opened. Expecting to find an indulgent Roseanne waiting for them, Amanda was dismayed to see her mother, instead. What a terrible day for Eleanor to come home earlier than expected!

Eleanor's eyes widened as they went from her dripping grubby grandson to their equally damp disheveled houseguest. "What in the world . . . ?"

"Aubrey was just showing me the creek," Jon said smoothly. "You have a nice place here, Eleanor. You must be very proud of it."

"You're soaked—both of you!" Eleanor exclaimed, unswayed by the flattery. "Aubrey, get in here right away. You'll catch your death of cold standing out in that cool air in wet clothes. Amanda, I can't imagine what got into you, letting him get in this condition. You know how delicate he is. It'll be a wonder if we don't have to take him to the doctor tomorrow because of this. And Jonathan, you should know better than to risk reinjuring your leg. I'm sure your mother would be very put out with you for taking such a reckless chance. Roseanne, bring towels, please. Quickly."

Amanda could almost see Aubrey getting smaller as Eleanor scolded. "I'm sorry, Grandmother," he said in the polite too-old voice Amanda was accustomed to hearing from him. "I didn't mean to worry you."

"Honestly, Mother," Amanda complained, thoroughly annoyed with Eleanor for ruining the one time she had seen Aubrey relaxed and happy and aware that Jon had begun to scowl. "It's nearly seventy degrees outside. A wade in the stream won't bring on pneumonia or any other horrible illness. Aubrey isn't delicate. He's a perfectly healthy boy."

She thought she saw a fleeting expression of gratitude in her nephew's face before Roseanne swooped down on them. The housekeeper distributed towels with characteristic nonchalance, making teasing comments about how "boys will be boys" and promising a hearty dinner, since she was sure they'd worked up quite an appetite. Her attitude was exactly what the situation called for, but Aubrey didn't respond. Amanda knew she had her mother to blame for that, since Eleanor was still standing nearby, wearing a look of displeasure she aimed equally at her daughter, grandson and houseguest.

"Whew," Jon muttered as soon as Eleanor had swept Aubrey off to change into dry clothes. "Your mother's not too happy with me right now. Guess I screwed up."

"Don't be silly. Aubrey was having a wonderful time with you. I'm sorry Mother overreacted like that—she's just not used to having a little boy in the house," Amanda said.

Jon, who was bending to rub the towel over his wet jeans, looked up with a lifted eyebrow. "She had a son of her own, didn't she?"

Amanda was swept with a sudden unexpected wave of grief. She swallowed hard, blaming an eventful afternoon for her emotionalism. "Yes, of course. But Jerome was . . . never a typical little boy. He was always very quiet, very serious. Much like Aubrey."

"Aubrey," Jon said, straightening abruptly, "needs to be encouraged to be a typical little boy. You saw how much fun he was having at the creek. He can't spend his whole childhood locked in his room with his books. It isn't natural."

Amanda couldn't help stiffening. "You made your opinions about the way we're raising him perfectly clear at lunch."

Jon held up a conciliatory hand. "I'm not trying to lecture you again. God knows your mother does enough of that. I was just making a comment."

"I know," she said with a faint sigh. "Come on, I'll help you to your room so you can change for dinner."

"I'm quite capable of—"

"Shut up, Jon," she said crossly, taking his rigid arm. "Stop being Mr. Macho for a few minutes and let me give you a hand, will you? I've had just about enough out of you for a while."

Startled into compliance, he went along with her, though he resisted leaning against her even when he began to limp badly. He refused the elevator, climbing the stairs slowly and carefully, bracing himself on the polished cherry bannister. When they passed Aubrey's room Amanda listened but could hear no voices coming through the closed door, so she assumed Eleanor had left the boy to change in peace.

Without speaking, Amanda moved to go to her room, but Jon detained her with a hand on her arm. "Amanda."

"Yes?"

"A.J.'s not the only one who needs to loosen up a little."

She frowned. "Now you're going to start telling me how to live *my* life?"

"No," he said with an impatient shake of his head. "I'm just saying it wouldn't hurt you to have fun sometimes, too. Seems to me this household could use a little more laughter."

She was too weary to argue with him. Shrugging off his hand, she took a step away before saying, "Thank you for your advice, Jonathan. I assure you I'll give it the consideration it deserves. I'll see you at dinner."

"Dammit, Amanda . . ."

But she didn't give him time to finish the complaint as she set off down the hall. She needed some time alone. Time to think about her feelings about Aubrey, about her mother—and about Jon. Time to think about what her life had become—and what she wanted to do about changing it.

And she was in desperate need of a relaxing mental trip to Tahiti just about now.

THE HOUSEHOLD TURNED IN early that night, after a quiet stilted dinner during which Jon, Amanda and Aubrey listened to Eleanor complain about the appalling social evils of the modern world. Amanda had remained silent for the most part, lost in her convoluted thoughts. Aubrey, too, had said little, his face bland and expressionless—except when he'd looked at Jon. Amanda hadn't missed the glowing hero worship in the boy's eyes, and she worried that Aubrey would be more withdrawn than ever when Jon had to leave.

She didn't believe she'd made any great strides with the boy that afternoon. She remembered Jon's comments at lunch, about how Aubrey was starving for attention, longing to be treated like a normal boy, rather than a delicate little genius. She knew he was probably right, especially after seeing the way Aubrey responded to Jon, but could she ever reach the boy the way Jon had? Had the patterns they'd established become so deeply ingrained that Aubrey would never learn to open up to her? Would Jon's departure merely drive another wedge between the two of them?

Unable to sleep, she decided to slip down to the kitchen for something to drink. Milk, perhaps, or juice, she thought, anything to soothe her mind and help her relax. Help her forget—at least for a few minutes—about the disturbing, unpredictable, thoroughly fascinating man sleeping down the hall.

But Jon wasn't sleeping, she discovered when she entered the kitchen. He was sprawled in a chair, wearing only a pair of jeans, finishing a glass of milk and absently massaging his outstretched right leg as he read a newspaper spread out on the table in front of him.

"Jon?" she asked, moving toward him. "Are you all right? Is your leg hurting you?"

He shook his head and stopped the massage. "It's just a little stiff. It'll be good as new before long. What are you doing up at midnight?" he asked. "Couldn't you sleep?"

"I was thirsty."

"I can recommend the milk. It's a very fine vintage. Day before yesterday, I think."

She smiled and opened the refrigerator. "Then I should definitely try it. Want some more?"

"Sure. You suppose Roseanne has any junk food hidden in this kitchen? I could go for a midnight snack."

"My mother would never allow Roseanne to bring junk food into this house," Amanda answered loftily.

He sighed. "I should have known."

"I, however—" she opened a pantry and reached behind a sack of flour on a high shelf "—have been known to sneak in an occasional box of fudge-dipped Oreo cookies." She produced the box with a smug smile. "It's my opinion that if you're going to indulge, it should be with something as rich and calorie-laden as possible."

Jon's eyes lit up. "I think I'm in love."

She made a face at him and set the cookies on the table between them as she slid into a chair. "Cupboard love. I can get that from a stray dog."

His eyebrow lifted wickedly. "I can give you something you wouldn't get from a stray dawg," he murmured, gently mocking her Southern accent.

"Fleas?" she suggested sweetly.

"Very funny."

"It was rude of me, wasn't it? Must be the company I've been keeping lately."

He shook his head. "Just open the cookies, will you?"

There was something disturbingly intimate about knowing the rest of the household slept while she and Jon sat alone in the kitchen, she in her robe and nightgown, he in nothing but jeans. She found herself admiring his chest from beneath her lashes as she handed him two of the cookies across the table. Their fingers brushed when he took them and a strange tingle coursed through her. Odd, she thought. She couldn't remember ever feeling quite like that in response to a casual touch before.

"Amanda—"

A sound from the doorway startled Jon into silence. Amanda looked around quickly, afraid they'd been caught by her mother. Now why should that possibility make her react with a guilty start? she asked herself in annoyance even as she identified the intruder. "Aubrey? What are you doing up? Is something wrong?"

The pajama-clad boy entered the kitchen hesitantly, his eyes rounded and curious. "I thought I heard something downstairs," he explained. "When I went to tell Jon, I found his room empty."

"So you thought you'd come down and investigate? Very brave of you," Jon told him, drawing his hand away from Amanda's. "Want to join us?"

Aubrey looked at Amanda, as if worried she'd send him straight back to bed. Instead, she smiled and stood, not sure whether she was relieved or disappointed that the spell between Jon and her had been broken. "I'll get you a glass of milk."

Jon pushed the box of cookies toward Aubrey as the boy took a seat at the table. "Here you go, A.J. Dive in."

"I'm not supposed to have snacks between meals— except a light snack after school," Aubrey answered politely.

Had the rules of this household really gotten so rigid? Amanda asked herself in response to the meaningful glance Jon sent her way. She shook her head. "An occasional snack won't hurt you, Aubrey, as long as you eat a well-balanced diet the rest of the time. Have a cookie. Two, if you like."

His eyes brightening, Aubrey took two cookies and accepted the milk from Amanda. "Thank you."

"You're welcome." She was a bit concerned about his being up so late on a school night, but there was no way she was going to mention that at the moment.

Jon kept up a low-voiced running monologue during the next twenty minutes or so, making Amanda and Aubrey smile and occasionally have to stifle a laugh. Amanda couldn't remember the last time she'd felt more comfortable and relaxed in her mother's home. Not within the past five months, at least. Aubrey, too, seemed more content than usual. What magic did Jon work with him? And with her, for that matter?

It was Jon who brought the interlude to an end, though Amanda had been on the verge of doing so herself, after seeing Aubrey yawn a second time in as many minutes. "We'd better turn in," Jon said, pushing his chair away from the table. "You have school tomorrow, A.J., and your aunt has to work."

"What are you going to do tomorrow, Jon?" Aubrey asked, obediently standing and carrying his empty milk glass to the sink.

"The security system your grandmother ordered is being installed tomorrow. Guess I'll hang around and supervise."

"I'd rather stay here and watch than go to school," Aubrey said wistfully.

Jon smiled and shook his head. "I'll show you how everything works when you get home, okay?"

"Okay."

"Right. Now kiss your aunt and you can walk me back to my room and tuck me in."

Aubrey giggled at the suggestion that Jon needed to be tucked in, though the casual order to kiss his aunt had him eyeing Amanda with shy uncertainty. She held out her arms. After only a slight pause, Aubrey stepped up to her and lifted his face. Swallowing a lump in her throat, Amanda brushed her lips across his cheek and gave him a quick warm hug. He didn't respond, exactly, but for the first time he didn't stiffen at her touch. She was grateful for even that slight sign of progress.

"What about you, Jon?" Aubrey stunned her by asking with a hint of mischief in his young voice. "Aren't you going to give her a good-night kiss?"

Surely Aubrey wasn't going to start matchmaking, Amanda thought with a silent moan. He was probably too young to understand that his aunt and his new hero were obviously mismatched. "Aubrey," she began, but Jon interrupted with a chuckle.

"This is one opportunity that's just too good to miss," he proclaimed, advancing on Amanda with a piratical gleam in his emerald eyes.

She took a step backward. "Uh, Jon—"

He had her bent back over his arm before she could finish the sentence. The loud smacking kiss was dramatic, and utterly chaste—staged entirely for Aubrey's amused benefit. So why was Amanda a quivering mess when Jon set her back on her feet and bade her a cheery good-night?

Telling the others she'd stay behind for a moment to hide the evidence of their midnight snack, she sent them on to bed. The moment they were out of sight, she pressed both hands to her pounding heart and took a long deep gulp of air. Her lips still tingled from Jon's kiss—no matter what the intent behind it!

8

IT WAS VERY LATE Thursday evening when Terry dropped Jon off at the foot of the steps leading up to the front entrance of the Hightower home. Terry had been an entertaining companion for a night of soul food and blues, and they'd had a good time.

They'd even shared ideas on who might be behind the kidnapping attempts. Terry leaned strongly toward Worley, who'd apparently treated Terry with open disdain on more than one occasion. Jon wouldn't have been surprised if the whole thing had been McFarland's idea, but he would rather have blamed it on Miller. He hadn't liked Amanda's ex-fiancé at all. Maybe because he truly hated the idea of Amanda's being that close to the jerk.

Jon had thoroughly enjoyed the evening, except for the way his thoughts had kept turning to Amanda— wondering what she was doing, whether she missed him at dinner, whether she liked soul food and blues as much as he did. What was going on here, anyway? He didn't know if she was capable of the warm caring feelings he most valued in a relationship, yet he found himself getting more and more involved with her. *Not smart, Luck. Real stupid, in fact.*

Jon climbed the stairs, noting with some satisfaction that it was getting easier to do so every day. Despite the workout he'd given it in the brief fight with McFarland and in the stream the afternoon before, it was healing rapidly. Wouldn't be long until he was fit to be back at work, he told himself, his thoughts drifting to Seattle and the familiar routines that awaited him there.

The thought of returning to his empty apartment gave him a sudden hollow feeling in his chest. Odd. He liked his place, liked his job, liked his life. Nothing had changed significantly during the past few days in Memphis. Had it?

He pushed the uncomfortable thoughts aside and he checked the security-alarm box neatly installed beside the front door. Good. Everything properly set. And the newly restored gate had been closed and locked, the security system functional there, as well. Amanda and Eleanor had apparently paid close attention to the instructions he'd given them before he'd set out for the evening on the town with his new friend. He punched in the designated numbers before opening the door with the key Eleanor had given him. Inside the house, he reset the alarm system before turning for the stairs.

The house was quiet. Though it was barely midnight, he assumed everyone was sleeping. He made no noise as he climbed the stairs. When he reached the top, some impulse made him look toward Amanda's room. Her door was closed, but a thin slash of light defined the bottom of it. She was awake, then.

He took a step toward his own room, then stopped. *Go to bed, Luck*, he ordered himself when his eyes turned back toward that beckoning slit of light. *You don't need this. And neither does she.*

Maybe he would have listened to his common sense if he hadn't caught the faint strains of music coming from her room. The barely audible melody acted like a magnet, drawing him slowly down the hall. He told himself he wouldn't disturb her; he only wanted to satisfy his curiosity about what sort of music she listened to alone in her room at night.

Classical, he realized a moment later without surprise. He'd have chosen blues or mellow jazz at this hour, but this seemed more fitting for Amanda. He tapped on her door without giving himself time to think about his actions.

The door opened after only the slightest pause. "You didn't even ask who it was," he reminded her, drinking in the sight of her with her rich auburn hair tumbled around the shoulders of her white satin robe.

"I didn't have to," she murmured, eyeing him with a mixture of wariness and curiosity. "Is there something I can do for you?"

Oh, yeah, he thought with a mental groan. He noticed how closely the thin robe was molded to her slender curves. Oh, did he notice. "I, uh, needed to talk to you a minute. Ask your permission about something."

Her brow lifted. "*My* permission?"

"Yeah. It's about Aubrey."

"Maybe you'd better come in," she said, moving out of the doorway. "After disturbing him last night, I don't want to wake him tonight."

"Oh. Right." *This was a dumb idea, Luck. Really dumb.* But he went into the room, anyway, and closed the door quietly behind him.

Amanda stood a few feet away from him, her hands clasped in front of her, her eyes darting skittishly from the turned-down bed to the room's only chair. "Um...sit down," she said. "I'll just turn the music off."

"No, leave it on. It's nice. Mahler's Ninth, right?"

"Yes." She seemed surprised that he could identify the music.

"Kind of sad, isn't it? He wrote more upbeat pieces."

"This suited my mood tonight."

He'd moved closer to her. They stood only inches apart now. Amanda had to tilt her head back to look up at him. He couldn't resist reaching up to touch her soft cheek. "Were you feeling sad tonight, Amanda?"

"Not . . . sad," she whispered, her breath catching when his thumb moved lightly over her lower lip. "Just a bit melancholy."

When he lifted his other hand to frame her hair fell softly over his fingers. "Want to talk about it?"

The breath she drew in was tremulous. Her hands fluttered at her sides, uncertainly, then rose to rest lightly against his chest. He wondered if she could feel his heart pounding through his white cotton shirt.

"Talk about what?" she asked, obviously struggling to concentrate on the conversation.

He brushed his lips against her temple, the touch so fleeting he hardly had time to taste her. He didn't dare allow himself more. Not yet. His voice was husky when he spoke. "About whatever is making you melancholy."

Her swallow was just audible. "No."

The music flowed around them, the heartbreaking notes trembling in the air. Amanda's eyes, wide open now, locked with his. In hers was the awareness of what was happening between them, of the magnitude of that development.

He wondered what she saw in his eyes as she searched them so thoroughly. He wasn't sure he could have defined his own emotions at that moment.

Whatever she saw in his eyes seemed to give her the encouragement to slide her hands up around his neck and burrow her fingers into the hair at the nape. Jon dropped his hands to her waist and pulled her closer until his mouth hovered above hers. "Amanda?" he murmured, not exactly sure what he was asking.

"Yes," she whispered.

"I hope that means what I think it does," he muttered, then covered her mouth with his before she had a chance to disillusion him.

Apparently she'd had no such intention. She responded to the kiss exactly as he would have wanted her to—with the fire and eagerness he'd caught hints of before. Only this time she didn't draw back, didn't withhold anything from him. This time she kissed him as though she'd been waiting as anxiously as he had for this glorious moment.

She felt so good in his arms, so right. The feelings she evoked in him were all new—and yet he felt as though he'd been waiting all his life to experience this.

He could feel her warmth through the thin satin of her robe, could almost feel her supple skin through it. But "almost" wasn't enough. He'd never wanted anything more than he wanted Amanda now. Slowly, to give her time to stop him, he slipped one hand between them and fumbled at the loose knot at her waist. To his overwhelming relief, she didn't resist.

The slippery fabric glided off her shoulders to pool at their feet, leaving Amanda clad in a matching white teddy. Lace and satin clung lovingly to her perfect breasts and slender hips and dipped in at her small waist. He'd never seen anything more lovely.

"You're beautiful," he muttered, then wished he could have thought of something more original. Something to express just how much this meant to him. Yet all he could do was repeat it, hoping she'd know what he was trying to say.

The room's soft lighting gave the deep shades in her hair a lambent glow as she tilted her head back to smile up at him. He filled his hands with the soft fragrant mass and held it as he captured her mouth with his own again. And again and again, until both of them were gasping for breath, both trembling with a need for more than kisses, more than the contact their clothing allowed them. By unspoken agreement, they moved toward the bed. Jon would have liked to lift her into his arms and lay her on the bed himself, but ruefully acknowledged that his leg would probably collapse beneath them if he tried. That was one romantic gesture that would have to wait a few weeks.

A few weeks? The phrase nagged at him with the knowledge that he wouldn't be here that long, that this could well be the only time he'd be with her like this. But he refused to allow that disquieting thought to linger; he refused to think beyond this moment, beyond this night. Tonight it was just Amanda and the music and this bed—and he intended to savor every moment.

IT HAD BEEN MORE than five long months since Amanda had done anything irresponsible, given in to impulse, lost herself in mindless pleasure. It had been even longer than that since she'd felt anything as wonderful, as exciting, as mind-shattering as Jon's embraces—or had she ever?

His body was hard, strong and tanned, his skin sleek and warm. She caught her breath at the sight of the ugly red scars marring his right leg, but he brushed off her concern and murmured reassurances between longer, deeper, hungrier kisses. His hands moved at her shoulders and the thin straps of her teddy fell away. Moments later he tossed the garment aside, baring her to his leisurely explorations. She arched into his hands and his mouth, dug her fingers into the pliant skin of his shoulders, gasped with delight at his skillful caresses.

She trembled when he brushed kisses over the hardened tips of her breasts, shuddered when he drew her deeply into his mouth. "Jon," she whispered breathlessly.

He lifted his head, his emerald eyes glowing as he looked down at her. "What is it?"

She shook her head against the pillows, suddenly unable to form a complete sentence. "I . . ."

His palm was warm against her thigh, his body pressed full-length to hers. She felt his heavy erection against her abdomen, felt the fine tremors running through him in response to the self-control he exerted, but his smile was gentle and patient. He wouldn't rush her, she realized gratefully. "I'm sorry," she murmured, reaching up to touch his flushed cheek. "I'm a little nervous."

"Is it too soon for you? Do you want me to go?"

She was pleased with the knowledge that he would go if she asked, that he wouldn't try to pressure her into more than she was ready to give. "No," she whispered, stroking the evening roughness on his jaw. "Don't go. I just want you to know this isn't something I do lightly—we haven't known each other very long." Five days, she thought wonderingly. He'd been in her life only five days. How could he have changed it so dramatically in such a short time?

He brushed a kiss across her lips. "Neither do I. I've wanted you from the moment you opened your door to me, Amanda. I've been going half-crazy with wanting you. But if it's too soon, if you're not ready, we'll wait."

"I don't want to wait," she whispered, pulling him back down to her. "I want you. Tonight. Now."

He groaned and covered her mouth with his own, his relief evident in the kiss. He would have stopped, she thought tenderly, but he hadn't wanted to. Neither did she.

Hesitance gone now, she abandoned herself to their lovemaking, kissing and caressing with an impatience that wouldn't be denied. Jon sensed her growing need, and felt that need himself. Their bodies moved as one, arching, rolling, shifting; their hands raced, stroking and clinging. They paused only long enough for Amanda to dig out a small box hidden deep in a drawer of her nightstand, and for Jon to don the protection she'd provided him, and then they were kissing again. They held each other tightly when he finally slipped inside her.

Amanda had a fleeting, half-formed thought that she'd suddenly become whole, suddenly discovered a part of herself that had been missing all her life, but then that fanciful notion was swept away in a deluge of pleasure so intense, so overwhelming, she could hardly breathe. She could only ride the waves, holding tightly to the man in her arms, clinging to his strength, his warmth, his encouragement, as reality shattered around her.

Jon made a choked sound that could have been her name. His arms tightened around her, driving the remaining air from her lungs, but she wouldn't have complained even if she'd had breath enough to speak. Her damp face buried in his corded throat, she continued to hold him even when his arms loosened, pulled her into the curve of his body and held her there while they both fell reluctantly back to earth.

JON COULDN'T HAVE SAID exactly how much time passed while Amanda lay tucked cozily into his shoulder, their legs entwined beneath the sheets. He was still in a rather dazed state, struggling to understand exactly what had happened between them. He didn't know quite how it had happened—he was sure he hadn't come to her room expecting this—but he didn't regret it. How could he? It had been the most amazing experience of his life!

"You asleep?" he asked, though he knew she was awake. She was so quiet, so still. Regrets? He hoped not.

"No," she murmured, her voice husky. "Just recuperating."

"Are you okay? I didn't hurt you or anything, did I?" he asked, suddenly worried that it hadn't been as perfect for her as it had been for him.

"You didn't hurt me," she assured him, finally lifting her head to look at him. He felt his breath catch in response to her smile. It was warm and tender and contented—and he hadn't realized until now how very much he'd wanted to see her smile just that way.

He tucked a stray strand of hair away from her eyes. "I really didn't come in here for this tonight. I'm not sure exactly what happened—but I'm glad it did."

"So am I," she whispered, and touched her lips lightly to his.

He was beginning to relax now, to accept that she really had wanted this as badly as he had—or almost, at least. It wasn't like him to be so anxious, so uncertain, after lovemaking, but then, with Amanda, he didn't feel quite like himself. He wasn't sure what the difference was, wasn't even sure he liked it, and couldn't imagine where this was all leading. But still, no regrets, he decided, tugging her back into his arms.

"You said you wanted to ask my permission about something," Amanda said.

He wondered why she'd suddenly changed the subject. Was she trying to avoid a discussion of this new development in their relationship? Was she as confused as he was? Probably. "Yes. Terry and I want to take A.J. and Terry's son, Nathan, to Overton Park after school tomorrow. You know, visit the zoo, check out the playgrounds, that sort of outing. Is it okay with you?"

"Aubrey and Terrence's son?"

The question disturbed Jon. He didn't like the possibility that the woman who'd taken him so close to heaven could be a snob. "Yeah. What about it?"

"Isn't Terrence's son quite a bit younger than Aubrey?"

"Only a few months. He's a fourth grader. Not a genius like A.J., I guess, but Terry says he's a good kid. I think the boys would enjoy it."

"You're welcome to ask him, of course," Amanda said hastily, as though she'd suddenly sensed Jon's growing displeasure with her. "I just...I mean, well...Aubrey hasn't shown much interest in children his age. I'm not sure he—"

"The kid needs some friends. His schoolmates are too old to want a nine-year-old tagging along with them. He's lonely."

"Don't you think I've known that?" she asked, and he couldn't miss hearing the pain throbbing in her voice. "I've tried to interest him in activities with children his own age, but he . . ." She paused to take a deep breath. "Maybe you'll have more success than I've had. Aubrey seems to value your input."

"I'm a novelty for him. We've talked about this, Amanda. He loves you. He just needs time to get to know you better. I've seen a lot of progress in the past couple of days."

"Have you?"

He looked down at the top of her head, wondering if he'd detected a note of sarcasm in the quiet question. Or bitterness, maybe? Did Amanda resent his efforts with Aubrey? He'd have thought she'd appreciate them, dammit.

And if she resented him, then how the hell was he supposed to interpret what had happened between them tonight?

"Amanda? Do you want me to back off with Aubrey? Want me to forget about the outing tomorrow?"

She shook her head against his shoulder. "No, of course not. It will be good for him to get out with someone his age."

"Then is it me? You ready for me to get out of your hair? The security system is installed and it seems to be a good one. There's really no reason for me to hang around any—"

"No!" She lifted her head so abruptly she nearly clipped him in the chin, "I don't want you to leave yet."

His ego swelled. "Well, I—"

"We still don't know who tried to kidnap Aubrey. What if they try again?"

His ego deflating like a popped balloon, Jon scowled. "Look, I told you from the beginning that I'm not here to make an arrest of the would-be kidnappers. That's up to the local cops. Your mother just asked me to research and recommend home security systems. I did that, and even oversaw the installation of the damned thing."

She touched his cheek, the gesture conciliatory. "I didn't mean to imply you haven't been helpful, Jon. You have, and I'm grateful. I'm just worried about Aubrey."

He couldn't hold a grudge in the face of that gracious apology. "I know," he muttered. "I understand. But try not to worry so much. Maybe they've given up now, after both their bumbling attempts failed. We have to assume they're not really professionals at this, to have screwed up so badly both times. They've probably abandoned the whole crazy scheme."

"I hope you're right," she said, though she didn't sound entirely convinced.

Neither was Jon, but he had no intention of letting her know that right now.

"Did you enjoy your evening with Terrence?" she asked, determinedly changing the subject again to avoid any more conflict.

"Very much. Terry's a nice guy."

"Yes, he is. I don't know what Mother would have done without him after my father died—before I moved back home."

"Did you enjoy having your own place?"

"Yes, I did," she answered, a touch of wistfulness coloring the words. "It was a small apartment, but I liked it."

"Why did you move back in with your mother?"

"For Aubrey's sake," she admitted. "When I found myself suddenly responsible for him, I realized how little I knew about raising children—as you've observed for yourself. My apartment was really too small for the two of us, and I didn't know what I'd do with him while I was working. I thought it would be better for both Aubrey and me if we moved in here where we'd have Mother and Roseanne and Terrence to help out."

Jon kept his own opinion of that move to himself, knowing he'd criticized her actions with Aubrey enough. Besides, he chided himself, what did *he* know about raising kids, especially a kid like Aubrey? No more than Amanda, really. In her shoes, he might have made the same decision she had.

"Did you know your brother had named you as Aubrey's guardian in his will?" he asked.

"No. I was stunned when his attorney informed me that I'd been named guardian and executor of the estate. We . . . we'd never discussed it."

Jon's arm tightened around her shoulders in response to the slight break in her voice. "Were you and your brother close?" he asked sympathetically, thinking of how close he was to his own brother and sister. It would break his heart if anything happened to either of his siblings.

Amanda sighed. "I wish we had been closer. Jerome and I didn't agree about much, but we loved each other. I suppose that's all that really mattered."

"What sort of things didn't you agree about?" Jon asked, curious to know more about Amanda and her family.

She shrugged, and he could feel her bare shoulder move against his hand. Absently he stroked her skin with his fingertips, enjoying the softness of her.

"Too many things to name briefly. He thought I should study harder, spend less time on frivolous pursuits like school dances and parties. Be a scholar. I wasn't. And when he finally accepted that I was never going to be an academic marvel like him, he thought I should do the 'sensible' thing and join my father in the banking business. He couldn't understand why I wanted to open a gift shop and sell knickknacks and gewgaws, as he called them. We quarreled a lot about that. And about Edward," she added, her voice falling a bit. "Jerome didn't care for Edward. Like Mother, he was opposed to the engagement."

Jon swallowed the words about Edward that automatically sprang to his lips. He could certainly understand why Eleanor and Jerome had disliked the guy. Instead, he said bracingly, "But Jerome trusted you enough to ask you to raise his son. He was showing an awful lot of confidence in you when he did that."

"I know." She nodded, her hair tickling his chin with the movement. "Though there are times I don't know if I was the best choice he could have made, it means a great deal to me that he trusted me that much. Aubrey was very important to Jerome and Wanda, my sister-in-law. I just hope I can live up to their confidence in me."

"You will," Jon assured her, brushing her hair out of his face. His fingers lingered in the soft thick mass. She shifted to a more comfortable position and he felt himself harden as bare skin glided against bare skin. He knew he should be getting back to his own room, knew Amanda wouldn't want anyone to suspect what had happened between them, but he found himself reluctant to leave the warm intimacy of her bed.

The music had stopped and the silence almost shimmered with mutual desire. Amanda looked up at him, her eyes going dark, her lips parting slightly. He slipped a hand into the hair at the back of her head and brought their mouths together. This kiss was gentle, less urgent than their earlier lovemaking. Jon took his time, savoring and exploring every centimeter of her mouth before slowly moving his attention elsewhere, with Amanda's full cooperation....

It was very late, almost dawn, when Jon finally slipped out of Amanda's bed and down the hall to his own. He'd left her sleeping deeply, exhausted by their loving. She hadn't even stirred when he'd lightly kissed her faintly swollen lips before leaving her.

As he fell heavily onto his own bed, he was more than half-asleep himself, too weary to dwell on how his life had suddenly changed now that he and Amanda Hightower had become lovers.

"No, I DON'T USUALLY carry that series of collector plates," Amanda informed a hopeful shopper Friday afternoon, "but I can order them for you," she added when the woman registered disappointment.

The woman's dark eyes brightened. "You can? Oh, that would be wonderful. The one I want is number four in the series—it's the only one I don't have, and I haven't been able to find it anywhere."

"Just leave me your name and phone number and I'll let you know as soon as it arrives," Amanda promised.

She finished making a notation of Mrs. Cameron's special order and slipped the pad beneath the counter. When she looked up a familiar face was smiling at her. She jumped. "Edward! You startled me."

Her ex-fiancé immediately looked contrite. "I'm sorry, dear. I thought you knew I was here."

"No. What can I do for you?" She hoped he wasn't there to ask her to dinner, a definite possibility since closing time was only fifteen minutes away. She didn't want to offend him, but she had no intention of having dinner—or anything else—with Edward tonight. Though it rather embarrassed her to admit it, even to herself, she had been counting the minutes all day until she could be back home. With Jon.

"Tomorrow is Delia's birthday," Edward explained, naming the efficient, indispensable secretary of the university sociology department. "I should get her something, but you know how inept I am at that sort of thing. I thought perhaps you could help me."

She smiled. "This *is* a gift shop, Edward. Of course I can help you."

His eyes held a warmth that made her uncomfortable. "I knew you could, dear. What would I ever do without you?"

She cleared her throat. "I've just gotten some lovely perfume bottles in. And a selection of nice porcelain music boxes. Do you think she'd like either of those?"

"A music box would be nice, I think. Why don't you choose one? After all, you know Delia. You probably know best what would appeal to her."

"I've only met her a couple of times, Edward," she reminded him dryly as she walked around to the display of music boxes. She picked up a delicate porcelain rose that played a few bars of "The Rose" when a tiny hidden key was turned. "How about this one?"

He glanced at it without much interest. "Yes, that will do. Perhaps you could wrap it for me?"

"Of course."

"And afterward, I thought perhaps we could—"

Amanda prepared herself for a tactful rejection to whatever plan he obviously had for the evening, but before he could finish the suggestion, Tricia interrupted by taking the music box out of Amanda's hand. "I'll wrap this for you, Dr. Miller," she offered brightly. "Amanda, it looks like your date for the evening is here."

"My date?" Amanda repeated blankly. "But—"

"Yes," Tricia said, still grinning as she moved toward the wrapping counter. "I just happened to notice two fine-looking gentlemen enter the store. Thought they might be looking for you. Or maybe I'll get lucky and they'll be here for me, instead."

Puzzled, Amanda looked up then. Her gaze locked with a pair of glinting emerald eyes. The intimacy she saw in his eyes sent waves of warmth rippling through her.

She swallowed. "Jon. And Aubrey," she added, suddenly noticing her nephew at Jon's side. "What are you two doing here?"

"We had Terry drop us off here after our park outing," Jon answered with a deceptively casual smile. "We thought we'd see if we could tempt you to join us for pizza and a movie tonight."

Amanda looked at her nephew. "Pizza and a movie, hmm?"

Aubrey nodded with just a trace of the old uncertainty, though he was looking at her with more confidence than he'd shown in the past, she noted with pleasure. "Yes, ma'am. Jon said he thought you might like a night out."

She wouldn't have quelled the anticipation in the boy's eyes even if she'd wanted to. "That sounds like fun. I'd love to join you."

Edward cleared his throat, a sound Amanda recognized as one of displeasure. She swallowed a groan and turned back to him. "Edward, you remember our, um, houseguest, Detective Luck?"

"Yes, of course," Edward said with even less enthusiasm than he'd displayed for his secretary's gift. He didn't extend his hand; nor did Jon. Neither man smiled.

Edward turned, instead, toward the boy. "Hello, Aubrey," he said in that too-bright voice some people inevitably used with children. "And how are you this afternoon?"

"Fine, thank you, Dr. Miller," Aubrey answered without inflection.

"Having an afternoon out with the bodyguard, are you?"

Aubrey blinked behind his glasses, as though wondering how to respond to the the rather barbed question. Jon's eyes narrowed.

Amanda stepped in quickly. "Jon is a visitor in our home, not a bodyguard," she said. "He and Aubrey have become good friends."

"How nice," Edward murmured, though the words hardly matched his expression.

"Here you go, Dr. Miller," Tricia said, reappearing with a beautifully wrapped package in her hands. "If you'll step over to the register, I'll take care of this for you. Amanda, I'll lock up this evening. You go on and have a good time."

"You're sure you don't mind? Jon and Aubrey can wait a few minutes—"

"I don't mind at all," Tricia cut in with a smile. "I had to leave early twice last week, remember? I owe you a few. Go on. Have fun. I'll see you in the morning."

"Amanda," Edward said, "I was hoping that you and I could—"

Amanda pretended she hadn't heard. "Be sure and tell Delia happy birthday for me, will you, Edward? I hope she likes the gift."

Jon reached out and took her arm, tugging slightly. "Ready to go?" he asked, and the undertone in his voice warned her that he'd been patient with her—and with Edward—for as long as he intended to be.

"Yes. I'm ready."

He barely gave her time to snatch up her purse before he urged her out the door. She could feel Edward's frowning gaze on her all the way out.

9

AMANDA GAVE THE KEYS to Jon and climbed into the front passenger seat of her car. It was easier to talk to her companions when she wasn't concentrating on traffic. And she wanted to talk to them, particularly to Aubrey.

Odd, she thought as she snapped on her seat belt, that it had taken a kidnapping attempt and a visit from a total stranger to wake her up to the realization that she'd nearly given up establishing a relationship with the boy.

Eleanor would probably be stunned to realize how many changes had taken place in her household as a result of her conversation with her old friend Jessica Luck.

Amanda gasped. "I forgot to call Mother to tell her we won't be home for dinner tonight! She'll be—"

"Already taken care of," Jon assured her with just a touch of smugness. "I told Roseanne this afternoon that A.J. and I were taking you out tonight. She said she'd just make a light dinner for your mother."

"Awfully confident that I'd say yes, weren't you?" Amanda challenged him, secretly relieved that she wouldn't have to confront her mother just yet.

"Hopeful, not confident," her lover corrected her.

She couldn't help frowning a bit at what she had called him in her mind. Her lover. Was that what Jon was? Technically, maybe—at least for one night. But now what?

"Did you enjoy your outing at the park?" she asked Aubrey to distract herself with an innocuous subject. She turned to look over the back of her seat at him, finding him intently watching her and Jon.

"Yes, ma'am. It was fun," he said, smiling at Jon with an affection she still couldn't help envying. "Wasn't it, Jon?"

Jon smiled into the rearview mirror. "Yeah. We had some laughs. Nathan's a real clown. Never stops cracking jokes."

"Do you like Nathan, Aubrey?" Amanda asked, wondering how the boys had gotten along.

"Yeah he's okay," Aubrey answered with the studiously casual tone boys used to mask more earnest feelings. "He's a lot like Terry, uh, Terrence."

"That's nice. Maybe you can get together again soon."

"Yes, ma'am. Maybe."

"Tell me about your afternoon," she encouraged him. "What all did you do?"

Aubrey responded with encouraging enthusiasm.

It was still a bit early for the pizza parlor to be crowded, so they didn't have to wait for a table. Jon and Aubrey both declared they were starving after their afternoon in the park, so they ordered a deep-dish pizza-with-everything.

Amanda insisted on adding salads to the order. Aubrey didn't protest—he liked salad. Jon, however, made a show of complaining about "rabbit food" and muttering about "healthy stuff." Amanda couldn't resist needling him when he made a second trip to the all-you-can-eat salad bar. Aubrey didn't say much, but seemed to enjoy the adults' teasing.

Never once did Jon mention finding Amanda's former fiancé at her shop when he'd arrived. Amanda thought the omission was quite deliberate—and rather pointed. Still, she didn't want to talk about Edward, either. Tonight was about her and Jon and Aubrey.

After dinner, they selected a relatively tame comedy movie with a PG rating. Aubrey sat between the two adults in the theater, a huge tub of buttered popcorn in his lap, which they all shared. Amanda tried not to think about the calories and fats they'd consumed that evening. She decided it didn't matter when Aubrey burst into giggles at a particularly silly slapstick scene in the movie.

Jon draped a casual arm over the back of Aubrey's chair, but his fingertips brushed Amanda's nape in a way that wasn't casual at all. She found it very hard to concentrate on the improbable plot of the film after that.

"I have to go to the bathroom," Aubrey whispered to Amanda the moment the film ended. "I don't think I can wait until I get home."

She hid her smile. "You can go on your way out of the theater. The bathrooms are in the lobby."

He nodded in relief. Jon offered to accompany the boy into the bathroom, but Aubrey was so embarrassed at the suggestion that he wasn't old enough to go by himself that Jon quickly backed down. Nevertheless, he kept a close eye on Aubrey as he pushed through the door to the men's room. But after all, what could happen? She and Jon were only a few yards away. She glanced at Jon with a forced smile. "It's difficult at times to keep from damaging his fragile pride," she agreed. "He's so sensitive."

"He seems to be getting over the kidnapping attempt without any lasting trauma." Jon commented. "I haven't heard him muttering in his sleep during the past couple of nights, so I think the nightmares have stopped."

Amanda sighed gratefully. "I hope you're right. I can't imagine how frightening that must have been for him. It's helped that you've been here," she added. "You've become his hero, you know."

Jon muttered something unintelligible and shifted his weight. Amanda smiled at his discomfort.

Her smile vanished when she heard Aubrey cry out.

She turned hurriedly, but Jon was already lunging toward the boy, who had been stopped outside the men's room by a chubby blond woman who had grabbed his shoulder. "Stop!" Jon yelled, drawing the attention of everyone in the crowded lobby. "Get away from that boy!"

The woman squealed and raised her plump hands in fright as she found herself confronted by a menacing-looking man and a frantic-looking woman. Amanda put both arms protectively around Aubrey and pulled him close. Jon faced the woman, his face darkened by a scowl. "What is it?" the woman asked hysterically, her round face drained of color. "What did I do?"

"Why don't you tell me?" Jon demanded.

"My little boy's in the rest room. I just wanted to ask your . . . your son to check on him for me. I—"

A little boy of about six or seven came through the men's room door, saw Jon looming threateningly over his mother and promptly burst into noisy protest. "Hey! You leave my mom alone!"

By now the worried theater manager had arrived to find out what was going on.

"That's not the same woman from the library," Aubrey announced in a small voice, looking tearfully up at Amanda. "I thought it was. I'm sorry."

Amanda tightened her arms. "It's okay, love. I understand."

"You're sure she's not the same one?" Jon asked carefully. "Look at her closely, Aubrey."

Aubrey peeked at the woman from within the circle of Amanda's arms and shook his head. "She's not the same one."

Jon relaxed visibly. He turned back to the distraught woman and the theater manager. "Someone tried to kidnap my son a few days ago," he said smoothly, letting the woman's assumption stand. "He's still nervous about it, as I'm sure you can understand."

"Kidnap? Oh, my heavens, how awful! Are you all right?" the blond woman asked Aubrey, clinging protectively to her own son. "I didn't mean to frighten you. I'm so sorry."

Jon quickly ushered Amanda and Aubrey out of the theater, away from the curious gazes of the spectators.

"You okay, A.J.?" he asked the moment they'd closed themselves into the blessed privacy of Amanda's car.

"I'm okay," Aubrey answered with a sigh. "I'm sorry I made such a scene."

"You did exactly the right thing," Jon told him firmly. "Anytime some stranger touches you, you yell out, you hear? Your safety comes first. Questions and explanations come later."

Aubrey nodded.

Though it wasn't particularly late, Aubrey fell asleep in the car on the way home, exhausted by the physical and emotional workout he'd had that day. Amanda looked over the back of the seat and murmured, "He's worn-out."

"Poor kid. I guess he's still more nervous about everything than we thought," Jon said in a low growl, glancing into the rearview mirror.

Amanda fought down a wave of anger at whoever had so callously frightened her nephew. What kind of person, she wondered grimly, would do this to a little boy who'd so recently lost both his parents? She tried to keep her voice even when she said, "I'm sure he enjoyed the day, though. It was nice of you to arrange everything for him. Outings like this probably do him good, if kept in moderation."

"Does that mean you'll make sure he has more outings like this?" Jon didn't look at her as he spoke, but she sensed that the question was more serious than his tone implied.

"Yes," she answered just as gravely. "He will have. I'll see to it."

"Good."

Amanda watched as he braked to avoid a slow-moving car, then moved his right foot competently back to the accelerator. "Speaking of overdoing it, how's your leg?" she asked, calling to mind a vivid picture of his scars—which, of course, led to memories of the rest of him unclothed. "You didn't push too hard today, I hope," she managed evenly, though with some effort.

"No. It's a lot better. I've always been a fast healer."

That wasn't all he was fast at, Amanda thought wryly, musing that he was the only man who'd ever gotten into her bed after so brief an acquaintance. Not even a week. She rode the rest of the way home pondering her uncharacteristic behavior.

Eleanor was waiting for them when they walked through the front door. Jon had an arm around Aubrey's shoulders, since the boy was still groggy with sleep. "Well," Eleanor said, looking from the boy's sleepy eyes to the tomato-sauce stain on his formerly neat white shirt. "It's about time you got home."

"Jon, would you see Aubrey up to his room, please?" Amanda asked, determined that Eleanor wouldn't spoil the child's evening any more than the incident in the theater had already done. "Aubrey, go ahead and get into bed. I'll be there in a few minutes to kiss you goodnight."

"Yes'm," Aubrey murmured, rubbing his eyes as Jon led him away. "G'night, Gra'mother."

"Wait, I . . ."

But Jon didn't give Eleanor time to finish the sentence. Without looking back, he guided the boy skillfully out of the room.

Eleanor whirled on Amanda. "I wasn't finished!"

"There was nothing else that needed to be said," Amanda replied simply. "At least, not to Aubrey. He's tired."

"He was obviously exhausted," Eleanor snapped. "He isn't used to staying out so late. He's only nine years old. Honestly, Amanda, how could you be so irresponsible?"

"One late night won't hurt him, Mother. Please don't overreact."

Eleanor drew herself up stiffly, frowning her displeasure at her daughter's tone. "I really don't know what's gotten into you lately, Amanda. You haven't spoken to me in that tone since you were a rebellious teenager."

"I'm sorry. I guess I'm tired, too."

Eleanor wasn't appeased. "I think I made a mistake by asking Jonathan to visit," she murmured. "This was obviously a bad time to bring an outsider into the household. Our routines have been upset and our household disrupted. We should have handled this situation ourselves—and we could have, for all that's been done."

"I'm sorry if I've disappointed you, Eleanor," Jon said from the doorway. "But if you'll remember, all I offered to do was help you select an adequate security system for your home. I'm not sure what else you expected from me."

Eleanor had the grace to look a bit embarrassed that Jon had overheard her criticism of him, but, she masked her discomfort with her usual cool dignity. "Of course we appreciate what you've done, Jonathan. I'm simply frustrated that no progress has been made in locating the people who attempted to kidnap my grandson. What if they try again?"

Amanda and Jon exchanged glances, and came to a mutual unspoken decision that Eleanor would not be told of the scare they'd received earlier. "Jon has done everything he can to make sure Aubrey is safe, Mother. We owe him our gratitude for coming all the way to Memphis just to do this favor for us."

"We *are* grateful, of course, Jonathan," Eleanor said, then added smoothly, "I'm sure you've done all you can for us. You must be impatient to get back to your own home and friends. When were you planning to go back?"

"Mother!" Amanda protested, appalled. But whether it was by her mother's barely masked impatience to be rid of Jon or her own dismay at the thought of his leaving she couldn't have said.

Eleanor gave her a look of bland innocence. "He's welcome to stay as long as he likes, of course. I just don't want him to feel obligated to stay. I'm sure he has an active social life back in Seattle. You must be impatient to return to it, aren't you, Jonathan?"

Jon spoke without expression, looking at Eleanor, rather than Amanda. "I thought I'd stay through the weekend to make sure the security system operates as well as it should. I'll probably head back to Seattle Monday morning."

Amanda's heart sank at his casual tone. Had it been his intention all along to leave so soon? If so, what had last night meant to him? Just a pleasant interlude during his visit to Memphis? It had been so much more for her.

She couldn't stand there any longer feeling trapped between her mother and Jon. Without looking at either of them, she headed for the door. "I promised Aubrey I'd kiss him good-night. And I think I'll turn in early, too. Good night, Mother."

"Amanda!" Eleanor obviously didn't consider herself finished.

"I said good night, Mother. We'll talk again tomorrow." Maybe by that time, she'd have her resentment under control, she thought tiredly.

Aubrey was in bed, the covers tucked to his chin, the room dark except for the night-light near the door. Thinking he was asleep, Amanda leaned over to press a kiss to his forehead. She was surprised when he spoke in a sleepy murmur, "Was Grandmother mad?"

"No, of course not," she lied without hesitation. "Did you have a good time today, Aubrey?"

"Yes. I had fun."

"Good. We'll do it again some time."

"That'll be nice." Aubrey's eyes fluttered, then closed. Smiling, Amanda brushed his hair back with a light touch and stepped away from the bed.

His eyes opened again, the lids heavy. "Aunt Amanda?"

"What is it, sweetie?"

"D'you think it would have been okay with my dad? That I didn't study today, I mean?"

Amanda's throat tightened. *Oh, Jerome, what did you—what did we—do to this child?* "Yes, darling. I think your dad would have approved of you taking an afternoon off from studying. Remember the chess tournaments he sometimes entered? That was his way of relaxing, taking some time away from work. And your mother liked to take long walks in the country. Remember?"

"Oh. Yeah. Then I guess it would've been okay with them."

"Your parents would have been very proud of you," Amanda said a bit thickly. "Just as I am."

His eyes closing, he murmured something unintelligible in response.

She had to wipe her eyes as she slipped quietly out of her nephew's room.

Jon was waiting in the doorway of his bedroom across the hall. "What's wrong?" he demanded, spotting her tears.

"Nothing." She changed the subject as she entered his room and turned to face him. "Jon, I'm sorry about the way Mother acted. She's just . . . upset over everything that's happened lately. She hasn't been herself since Jerome died."

He shrugged. "She doesn't bother me. You're the one who should be tired of being treated like an irresponsible kid. When are you going to get your own place again?"

Her eyes widened at the unexpected question. "I wasn't planning to move out anytime soon. Aubrey—"

"Aubrey would be better off without his grandmother breathing down his neck all the time trying to turn him into a reincarnation of his father," Jon said bluntly. "Don't use him as an excuse for your own cowardice, Amanda."

"Cowardice?" she gasped indignantly. "What are you talking about?"

"You're still afraid to take full responsibility for that kid," he said, not bothering to mince words. "Hell, you're trying as hard as A.J. to take Jerome's place for your mother. You have your own life to live, Amanda, and so does the boy. Don't let it slip away from you out of some misguided sense of duty. Your mother is fully capable of living her own life."

Amanda had had just about enough for one evening. Still shaken from the episode in the theater, her emotions still raw from the encounter with her mother, she felt her temper starting to rise. She drew herself up in an unconscious imitation of Eleanor at her most regal. "You were asked to give advice about our security, Jonathan. Not my personal life. I'm perfectly capable of making my own decisions in that regard, without any help from you."

His eyes darkened. Maybe his own temper had been frayed a bit tonight. "Yeah," he muttered. "I can see you've been doing a hell of a job so far."

She caught her breath. "Look, you have every right to be annoyed with my mother's rudeness earlier, but there is absolutely no call for you to take it out on me! I don't deserve your criticism."

"It's not criticism, dammit!" Jon retorted. "I just hate watching her treat you like that. And I don't like to think that after I leave Monday, everything's going to go back just the way it was before I got here. Haven't you noticed how different A.J. has been acting the past couple of days? Didn't you realize the kid's been miserable and lonely for the past five months—or more?"

"I'm well aware that you've swept in here and taken over my nephew!" she snapped, furiously blinking back tears of hurt at his cutting words. It was with great effort that she kept her voice low, since she was aware that Aubrey slept only a few yards away. "It's easy for you to spout advice. You'll only be here for a few more days, and then you'll walk away without even looking back. And how am I supposed to take your place with Aubrey, hmm? But why should you worry about that? It's not as if anything has changed for *you* during the past week!"

"Nothing's changed for me?" Jon repeated, looking incredulous. "What the hell do you think last night was all about?"

"You tell me," she answered stiffly. "A vacation fling? A one-night stand? Or maybe you thought you were doing me a favor. Was that it?"

A thin white line appeared around Jon's mouth. His green eyes snapped with a sudden show of temper that made Amanda take an involuntary step backward. "If that's what you think, maybe it *is* time for me to go," he said, the words low, clipped, precise.

"We've both known all along that you were only here for a brief visit," she replied, trying to keep her face impassive, trying to hide that her heart was breaking. What was she doing? Why was she trying to push him away? Did she really think it would be any easier to watch him leave if she was the one to bring their brief affair to an end?

"I'd like you to stay through the weekend as you'd planned," she added, holding herself together through sheer force of will. "It will be easier for Aubrey if he has time to prepare himself for your departure."

Jon nodded stiffly. "Right. And don't worry about me offering any more advice. I'll keep my mouth shut from now on."

"I'd appreciate it," she said coolly, turning toward the doorway. "Good night, Jon."

He grunted. She took that as a reply.

She waited until she'd closed herself in her own room before she fell apart. With her hands clenched in her hair, she collapsed onto the bed, closed her eyes and curled into a fetal position. What the *hell* had happened? she asked herself, feeling bruised and shaken by the sharp exchange. The evening had begun so pleasantly, so warmly—after the rather awkward beginning with Edward.

Had Edward's intrusive presence earlier had anything to do with the anger between Jon and her tonight? Was Jon feeling jealous, suspicious? Surely he knew there was no reason to!

Was she afraid of what would happen when this affair ended? Had she subconsciously compared her relief at the end of her engagement with the devastation she feared would follow Jon's departure?

Groaning, she buried her face in her pillow, knowing she'd find no answers to her questions tonight. She doubted she'd sleep at all. And if she did, she knew exactly who she'd dream about.

"Dammit, Amanda, what are you going to do now?" she asked herself aloud, the question echoing endlessly in the quiet, empty bedroom.

SATURDAY STARTED OFF badly and went downhill from there. Amanda hadn't had such a lousy day since the day she'd been informed that her brother and his wife had died in a car accident.

She crawled out of bed after a thoroughly miserable, near-sleepless night, tired and cross and dispirited. She slipped out of the house without seeing anyone and arrived at her shop a full two hours before opening time. Dusting merchandise for those two hours did little to brighten her mood.

Tricia arrived suffering from a sinus headache that made her quiet and withdrawn. Business was grindingly slow that morning, unusual for a weekend. And then Edward showed up again without notice and pressured Amanda into letting him take her out to lunch. She'd went simply because she was too weary to argue with him about it.

He spent the entire hour trying to persuade her to give their relationship another chance, making less than subtle attempts to find out about her relationship with Jon and offering unasked-for advice about Aubrey's safety and Amanda's life. She was getting heartily sick of unasked-for advice—as she finally informed him just before asking him to take her back to her office.

To top the afternoon off, she caught sight of Grady McFarland hanging around outside her shop late in the day. He didn't try to come in this time, thank heaven, but he made no effort to hide. As though he wanted her to know he was watching her.

If his intent was to make her nervous he did a damned good job of it. Both Amanda and Tricia found it difficult to concentrate on work with that lowlife hovering like a vulture just outside. Amanda finally called the police, who sent someone to warn him off. McFarland left with an obscene gesture for Amanda's and Tricia's benefit.

Amanda's head was pounding by the time she drove through the open gates of her home. Why had the gates been left open? she wondered, then groaned when the answer presented itself in the form of a familiar vehicle parked at the foot of the stairs. This was absolutely all she'd needed today, she thought with a groan. A visit from Howard Worley.

She was barely inside the door before she heard her name. Sighing, she replied, "Yes, Mother, I'm home. Hello, Howard," she added unenthusiastically as she entered the living room. Eleanor and Howard were perched stiffly on the edge of their chairs while Jon leaned against the marble mantel, his arms crossed belligerently over his chest.

Amanda could tell at a glance that Jon's temper had been pushed to the edge again. Giving him a cool nod of greeting, she took a seat. "Where's Aubrey?"

"He's outside, playing with the chauffeur's son while the chauffeur works on your car," Howard replied with a scowl. "Lacking friends of his own, he is reduced to socializing with the servants' children. If he lived with me, he—"

"But he doesn't live with you, does he, Howard?" Amanda interrupted sweetly, giving him a smile that showed all her teeth. "Terrence's son is a nice boy. He's a perfectly acceptable playmate for Aubrey."

"I haven't even had a chance to speak to my nephew this afternoon," Howard complained, giving Jon a seething look that spoke volumes.

He turned back to Amanda with his face set in a facsimile of reasonableness. "I was just explaining to Eleanor that my wife and I would like to have Aubrey as a guest for the weekend. I have tickets to the Memphis State game this evening, and Loretta and I thought we'd take him out to dinner afterward. He could attend church with us tomorrow morning and then return after lunch—if he wants to return that early. Eleanor has refused to even consider our request, but as I've pointed out, *you* are officially the boy's guardian. The decision is yours to make, not hers."

"And what makes you think mine will be any different?" Amanda asked with a lifted eyebrow.

"Because I think you are genuinely fond of the child," Howard shot back with an obvious attempt to appeal to her softer instincts. "You wouldn't refuse Aubrey a little fun just to spite me, would you?"

"Of course I wouldn't," Amanda assured him. She ignored her mother's sputter of protest and Jon's expressive grunt. "The thing is that I don't think Aubrey *would* have fun with you, Howard. I don't think he'd enjoy the weekend at all, since I'm absolutely certain you would use the time to browbeat him about coming to live with you, and to criticize the way Mother and I are raising him. My answer is no. He won't be spending the weekend with you."

Howard's plump cheeks flushed dangerously. "You aren't even going to ask the boy what he wants?"

"It isn't necessary. Aubrey would decline."

"Why don't you call him in and find out?" Howard challenged.

"I see no need to subject him to that unpleasant scene. You have your answer, Howard. You may visit with him for a few minutes before you leave if you like, but he won't be staying with you this weekend."

Howard shoved himself out of his chair and loomed over Amanda, fury hardening his expression. Amanda was aware that Jon had straightened, every muscle in his lean body poised for action if necessary. She gave him a quick warning glance before turning back to Howard. "You wanted to say something else?"

"Oh, yeah," he said between gritted teeth. "You're going to regret this, Amanda. It's not going to look good in court when I point out that you're deliberately alienating the boy from his own mother's family. If you think any judge is going to accept that, you have quite a shock coming."

"I'm not keeping you from Aubrey, Howard," Amanda pointed out, resisting an impulse to raise her hands to her throbbing temples. "As I've said, you're welcome to visit him at any time, though I would still ask that you call first. However, I won't force him to spend more time with you than necessary, nor will I subject him to your harassment for more than the duration of your brief closely supervised visits. I can't stop you from taking me to court, but I will continue to act in what I consider to be Aubrey's best interests, despite your threats."

"Listen, you snotty bitch, you—"

"All right, Worley, that's enough," Jon snapped, surging forward. "You're out of here."

Howard took an involuntary step backward. "Don't you—"

Terrence appeared in the doorway without warning, his dark eyes wide with concern. "Jon? It's the boys. I can't find them. They've disappeared."

10

FOR A SECOND, no one moved. Jon recovered first. "What do you mean you can't find them?"

Terrence made a despairing gesture with one hand. "They were playing back by the creek. When I went to collect Nathan, they were gone. I've looked all over the grounds. I can't find them anywhere."

"Have you checked Aubrey's room?" Amanda asked, stepping forward.

Terrence nodded. "Yes. They aren't there. And Roseanne hasn't seen them in the kitchen."

"Eleanor, you search the house," Jon ordered, moving swiftly toward the doorway. "The rest of us will look outside."

"Should I call the police?" Eleanor asked a faint tremor in her voice.

"Not yet," Jon answered without slowing down.

"I knew something like this would happen!" Howard blustered, moving toward the doorway. "If anything has happened to my nephew, I—"

With one foot already out in the hallway, Jon turned to face Howard, who stood less than a yard away from him. Amanda thought that even the bravest of men would have quailed beneath Jon's fierce gaze—and Howard was far from the bravest of men. "One more word out of you, Worley, and I'll shut your mouth for you," Jon warned in a tone too soft and steady to be taken for anything but absolute truth. "Is that clear?"

Howard subsided, glowering in resentment. Amanda wasn't surprised that he said nothing more.

Calling the boys' names, Jon, Terrence and Amanda searched the grounds, Howard tagging sullenly after them. Amanda's pulse was racing, her fear growing as the minutes ticked past. "The front gates were open when I drove in," she fretted to Jon. "Could someone have . . . ?"

She couldn't finish the sentence.

He reached out to squeeze her shoulder. "We'll find him, Amanda. Keep looking."

A hoarse shout from Terrence that came from the direction of the creek made Amanda and Jon spin that way. Amanda sagged in relief to see the two boys appear, rumpled and grubby, looking surprised at all the commotion. She reached her nephew before the others and hugged him tightly in sheer relief. "Thank God you're safe! Where have you been?"

Aubrey seemed startled by her fervor, but he didn't pull out of her arms. He looked up at her questioningly, suddenly suspecting he'd done something he shouldn't have. "We were on the empty lot on the other side of the fence," he explained. "We wanted to find the source of the creek. Did you know it comes from an underground spring about a hundred yards from our property line?"

"It's really cool, Miss Hightower," Nathan added earnestly. "See, there's this great big rock and a—"

"Didn't I tell you not to leave this property, young man?" Terrence interrupted.

Nathan's dark eyes were wide. "No, sir. You didn't."

Terrence let out an exasperated breath. "Well, I shouldn't *have* to say it! You should have known better."

"And so should you, Aubrey," Amanda seconded, though she couldn't make herself release him. "Don't you know how worried we were when we couldn't find you?"

Aubrey hung his head. "I'm sorry, Aunt Amanda. I wasn't thinking."

Howard swung an arm in a telling gesture. "This is just an indication that the boy needs activities more fitted to his age than those you've been providing for him," he lectured sanctimoniously. "If Aubrey were to live with *me*, he'd have plenty of activities to keep him out of mischief, as well as suitable playmates," he added, putting just enough stress on "suitable" to make Terrence stiffen angrily.

Aubrey, who had also stiffened at his uncle's words, looked up at Amanda in mute appeal. She gave him a reassuring squeeze, then smiled at his crestfallen playmate. "There's no harm done this time, boys. Next time you play together, please remember never to leave the grounds without permission."

"Yes, ma'am," the boys said in unison, darting looks of relief at each other.

"C'mon, Nathan, we're going home," Terrence told his son sternly, his displeasure softened by a gentle touch on the boy's shoulder.

"Yes, Dad. 'Bye, A.J.," Nathan said, then turned to Amanda. "Sorry we worried you, Miss Hightower."

Amanda gave him a reassuring smile as his father led him away, then squeezed her nephew's shoulder. "Go on in and clean up, Aubrey. Be sure and tell your grandmother where you've been. She's been worried."

"Yes, ma'am. 'Bye, Uncle Howard."

Howard frowned. "I'd like to talk to you before I leave, Aubrey."

Aubrey glanced up at Amanda, the appeal in his eyes unmistakable. It was the first time he'd looked to her for support against his uncle. She didn't let him down. "Some other time, Howard. A.J.'s tired and hungry. He needs to be getting ready for dinner."

The boy smiled at her use of his new nickname. She'd done so to emphasize the contrast between her and his disapproving uncle, and she believed she'd succeeded. Even Jon was looking at her with more approval than he had the night before. She told herself that his approval really shouldn't matter to her quite so much.

Before Howard had a chance to spew more protests, Jon took a step closer to Amanda. "Time for us to be getting ready for dinner, too," he said meaningfully. "I'm sure we'll be seeing you again, Worley."

"Now, wait a minute. You aren't dismissing me like some sort of—"

"Yes. He is," Amanda cut in flatly. "Goodbye, Howard. Call before visiting next time, or the security gates will probably not be opened for you."

"Why, you—"

"Don't push it, Worley," Jon advised quietly, looking as though he truly hoped the older man ignored the advice.

Howard wasn't that foolish. Quivering with outrage, he stormed away, muttering dire threats and promises.

"Oh, God," Amanda said with a weary sigh, pushing her hands through her hair. "What *else* can go wrong today?"

Jon hesitated only a moment before sliding a hand beneath her hair and squeezing her neck in a gentle massage. "Been a bad one, eh?"

"Lousy," she admitted, unable to prevent herself from arching into the delicious pressure of his fingers.

"I guess the way I acted last night didn't help...." He took a deep breath, and his fingers stopped their soothing motion. "Amanda, about what I said last night—I'm sorry. I was out of bounds. I had no right to criticize the choices you've made since your brother died. I know it hasn't been easy for you."

The lengthy apology took her by surprise. Disarmed, she stared up at him. "I..." Her voice died away as she fumbled for the right words.

He cupped her face between his rough hands. "I lay awake most of the night thinking about you. Calling myself a jerk for talking to you the way I did when I should have been telling you how special you are. Telling you that I know you've been trying with A.J. and that your efforts mean a lot to the boy. Telling you how damned beautiful and desirable you are. Can you forgive me for taking my irritation with your mother out on you?"

She slid her hands up his chest to rest on his broad shoulders. "Yes," she whispered, tilting her face up to his. "If you'll forgive me for doing the same thing."

"You've got it," he groaned. "Damn, I want to kiss you."

She rose on tiptoes and brought her mouth within an inch or so of his. "What's stopping you?"

His grin was a slash of white across his tanned face, and then his mouth was on hers and her eyes closed as she melted into the embrace.

Jon tangled one hand in her hair and used the other to pull her closer. With her arms locked around his neck Amanda strained against him, her lips parting to invite a deeper kiss. Jon accepted the invitation with a hungry passion that brought back memories of the night they'd spent together. Making Amanda ache for another night just like it—followed by many, many more nights of loving.

Was she being a fool to allow herself to dream of a future with him? At the moment she couldn't care less. She wanted him. She needed him. She strongly suspected that she'd fallen in love with him.

Jon's body throbbing against hers told her she wasn't the only one fantasizing about carrying the kiss further. "Amanda," he muttered between hot stinging kisses. "Oh, God, I want—"

"*Amanda!*"

Eleanor's sharp cry tore them apart as effectively as a bucket of ice water. Jon dropped his arms so suddenly that Amanda staggered a bit, but she caught herself and looked at her mother in exasperation. "Honestly, Mother, you scared me half to death."

"I would like to speak to you, Amanda. In private, please," Eleanor added with a cool glance at Jon.

He looked uncertainly from Amanda to her mother and back again, searching for a clue as to what Amanda wanted him to do. She straightened her hair with one unsteady hand and attempted a smile for his benefit. "I'm sure you'd like to freshen up for dinner, Jon. Go on in. Mother and I will be in shortly."

"You're sure?" he murmured, willing to stay for moral support if she asked.

She appreciated the gesture, but waved him on. "See you at dinner."

She waited until he'd moved out of hearing before turning back to her mother. "Why in the world did you shriek that way?" she asked bluntly, going on the offensive before Eleanor could do so. An old trick she'd learned as a teenager.

Eleanor's chin rose. "I do not shriek."

"You shrieked. And you were quite rude to Jon just now. Why?"

"I was taken by surprise," Eleanor admitted stiffly, lacing her hands together as she faced her daughter in much the same way as she had when Amanda had misbehaved as a child. "I certainly never expected to find you engaged in such an indiscreet ill-bred display of . . . of . . ."

· "Passion? Lust?" Amanda supplied, goaded into recklessness.

Eleanor harrumphed. "I don't know why I bother to talk to you sometimes. I thought you'd changed in the past few months. I thought you'd finally learned to accept your responsibilities to your family. But you're still as rebellious and headstrong as ever, aren't you?"

The words hurt, especially since Amanda had been trying so very hard during the past five months to live up to Eleanor's expectations. As she'd always done, she hid the hurt behind a defiant scowl. "I was kissing Jon, Mother, not desecrating the family name. As usual, you're exaggerating."

"I certainly hope you aren't considering a romantic liaison with that young man. It wouldn't do, Amanda. Not at all."

With massive effort Amanda kept her voice at a moderate level. "Surely you're not accusing Jon of being a fortune hunter, too? Not your own dear friend's son?"

"Of course Jessie's son isn't a fortune hunter. But he's been raised very differently from you, Amanda. He doesn't fit in here—nor would you fit in his world. There's no future in this, and you will only embarrass both our families if you continue to act so irresponsibly. You do have Aubrey to consider, you know. What sort of example are you setting for him with this behavior?"

"*I* will worry about the example I'm setting for A.J., Mother," Amanda replied, again using the nickname deliberately. "If you'll remember, I am his guardian, not you."

"A.J." Eleanor snorted delicately. "What a vulgar name. Having Jonathan come here was definitely a mistake. Sadly, he has turned out to be a bad influence on the entire household."

Furious for Jon's sake, Amanda snapped, "He has taken time out of his recuperation from a serious injury to offer his expertise to a household of strangers. He's befriended a lonely little boy who's been drawing further and further into himself for the past five months. And he's done so with very little thanks from anyone—including me, to my regret. I won't hear another word against him, is that clear, Mother?"

Eleanor let out an indignant breath. "At least he'll be leaving soon. Since I'm quite sure he has no intention of continuing this flirtation once he returns to his own pursuits in Seattle, I shall say nothing more about it. I just hope you don't regret your defiance once you have time to realize how foolishly you've been behaving with him."

Amanda swallowed the angry words trembling on her tongue, knowing she was perilously close to a temper tantrum like the ones she'd thrown as a frustrated mutinous adolescent.

Eleanor didn't wait for her to speak before bringing up her next complaint. "Your ex-fiancé was here this afternoon."

That news revived Amanda's power of speech. "Edward was *here?*" After he'd taken her to lunch? "Why?"

"He was very solicitous. He said he wanted to check on our welfare. He claimed he grew very fond of the family during your engagement and says he's been worried about us lately. He didn't stay long. Jonathan wasn't very gracious to him."

"I doubt that you were, either."

"I was perfectly polite," Eleanor rebutted coolly. "I just hope he doesn't make a habit of dropping by unannounced. If he does, you'll have to say something to him about it."

Since Amanda was well aware that her mother could be "perfectly polite" and still convey intense displeasure, she was sure Edward had gotten the message clearly enough. She sighed. Why didn't Edward give up? She didn't really believe he was suffering from unrequited love. Maybe Eleanor had been right all along. Maybe it *was* Amanda's money that Edward was having such a hard time giving up.

She waited until her mother had disappeared into the house before following, giving herself time to recover her poise. She wasn't entirely successful, perhaps because she didn't know how much her mother had said was true—about Edward *or* Jon.

Was she behaving foolishly? *Was* she starting to expect something from Jon that he never intended? Could she be falling in love with a man who was only amusing himself for a few days before returning to his own carefree life?

She groaned and headed determinedly toward her room. It would take more than a fleeting fantasy of tropical solitude to dispel this headache.

CLAIMING A HEADACHE of her own, Eleanor had a dinner tray sent up to her room. Amanda was relieved. She hadn't been looking forward to trying to eat with Eleanor watching every move she and Jon made.

Aubrey was quiet during the meal. That wasn't unusual for him of course, but Amanda thought he looked more subdued than usual. Jon seemed to agree. Both of them asked if anything was bothering him, but the boy assured them he was just tired. He excused himself soon after dinner, claiming he had homework to do before bedtime.

"Do you think your mother chewed him out for his disappearing act this afternoon?" Jon asked after Aubrey left them in the den where they'd settled after dinner.

"Probably," Amanda replied with a sigh. "I'll talk to him before he goes to bed, try to explain that what he did was wrong, but not terrible."

Jon started to say something, then stopped himself and turned his attention to the television guide, instead. "There's a music-awards show on. Want to watch it?"

"Not particularly. What were you going to say just now?"

"Nothing."

She shook her head with a faint smile. "Don't tell me that. You started to speak, then changed your mind. What was it?"

"I've made a vow—no more unasked-for advice."

"Then consider it asked for. What were you going to advise?"

He sighed and settled beside her on the couch. "I was just going to repeat that you and Aubrey would be better off living somewhere else. I'm sure your mother means well, but she hasn't a clue about raising a little boy. It can't be good for him to repress his own needs to try and live up to her expectations of him."

"I know," Amanda agreed with a sigh of her own. Was it because Jon was talking about her future without including himself in it? Or because she knew he was right? "It isn't good for Aubrey to live like this. I thought it would be easier for us here, but I was wrong, I guess. I don't know the first thing about being a single parent, but I think it's time for me to learn. I'll start looking for a place for us—as soon as I'm sure Aubrey will be safe."

Jon frowned. "You'd want a place with good security, of course. And he shouldn't be left alone much."

"I can afford good security, Jon. I have my own earnings, as well as the income from my inheritance. Aubrey won't be a latchkey child."

He grimaced apologetically. "I never meant to imply that he would be. Sorry."

"We seem to be doing a great deal of apologizing today."

His mouth twisted. "Yeah. Why don't we give it a rest?"

She smiled. "It's a deal."

He leaned over and kissed her lightly, sealing the pact. He didn't pull back far when he spoke. "Eleanor didn't like finding us together, did she?"

Amanda cleared her throat and looked down at her tightly linked hands. "No," she admitted. "Not particularly."

"Why not?"

"She thinks I'm behaving irresponsibly. Setting a poor example for Aubrey."

Jon swore under his breath.

"My mother is very old-fashioned in many ways, Jon. Don't let her bother you."

He shrugged. "As long as it doesn't bother you."

"I've learned to live with it. I've been making my own decisions about my social life since I was a teenager. I have no intention of changing that with now."

"Does that mean I won't be sleeping alone again tonight, despite your mother's disapproval?" He asked the question lightly, but she shivered at the hunger in his eyes.

"No," she whispered. "You won't be alone tonight."

He leaned toward her again.

She stopped him quickly by pressing a hand to his chest. "Not here. Let's go upstairs."

"Worried that someone will see us?" he asked, though he drew back as she'd requested.

She smiled and touched his cheek. "Worried that we'll be interrupted," she said.

His rakish smile of approval warmed her heart.

Jon offered to make sure the house was locked up and the security system activated while Amanda had a good-night chat with Aubrey. Afterward, he said, he wanted to stop by his own room for a shower. They agreed that he would join her in her room later.

Amanda left him with a kiss and a smile of anticipation.

She tapped on Aubrey's door and waited for him to speak before she entered. She found him sitting at his desk behind a pile of books. "How's your homework coming?"

"Almost finished," he replied, setting his pencil aside. "Just two more problems to do."

"Good." She sat on the end of his bed, her hands braced on either side of her, wondering how to begin. "Aubrey, about this afternoon . . ."

She saw him grow tense and anxious. "I'm really sorry I worried you, Aunt Amanda," he said hastily, looking at her with unmistakable pleading. "I won't ever do it again. Please don't send me to live with Uncle Howard. I'll be good if you'll let me stay with you."

Stunned, Amanda stared at him. "Send you to live with Howard? Aubrey, I'd *never* do that! What makes you think I would?"

"I know he's been trying to talk you into it," Aubrey replied miserably. "He said it would be better for everyone, especially you, if I went to live with him and Aunt Loretta. But I won't be any more trouble for you, Aunt Amanda. I promise."

"Aubrey, come here."

Hesitantly he stood and approached her. She waited until he was close before reaching out and pulling him into her arms for a firm loving hug. And then she held him a few inches away, her hands on his shoulders, her eyes locked with his. "I am *never* going to send you to live with Howard Worley. Do you understand? I love you, Aubrey. I want you to stay with me."

"Really?" He looked almost afraid to believe her.

"Really," she answered. "How could you ever believe differently?"

Aubrey hung his head. "I heard you talking to Grandmother after you found out you were my guardian. You said you didn't know anything about raising kids. You said you'd worked hard to make your own life away from your family and you didn't want to give up that freedom. And then you had to move out of your apartment because it wasn't big enough for me, and you broke up with your boyfriend because of me, and—"

"Now wait a minute," Amanda interrupted, sickened by the realization that Aubrey had thought she didn't want him. "My breaking up with Edward had absolutely nothing to do with you. I would have ended that relationship, regardless, because I realized I didn't love him enough to marry him."

"But I heard you talking to Grandmother...."

"I'm sorry you overheard that, darling," she said, drawing him down to sit beside her. "I probably did say those things, but I didn't really mean them—not the way it sounded, at least. I was overwhelmed by my grief and shock at your parents' death and by the responsibility of raising their child. I guess I was a little scared that I couldn't live up to their faith in me. Can you understand that?"

Aubrey nodded. "I think so."

"I know I haven't done a very good job of communicating with you since you came to live with me,

Aubrey. I haven't talked to you enough about what you wanted, what you were feeling. I didn't really know *how* to talk to you, and I think maybe you didn't know how to talk to me, either. I'd like for us to get beyond that, to learn how to talk to each other. To get to know each other better."

"I'd like that, too," he said shyly. "You really don't mind being responsible for me now?"

"I love being responsible for you," she assured him with another hug. "I love you, Aubrey. I always have and I always will."

"I love you, too, Aunt Amanda."

She rapidly blinked back tears at hearing those words from him for the first time. "When the police have finished their investigation—when we're absolutely sure you're safe—you and I are going to look for another place to live. Would you like that? We'll come visit Grandmother often, of course, but I think we'd do better on our own, don't you?"

Aubrey bit his lip. "Would Jon live with us?"

She caught her breath, then forced herself to release it slowly. Her smile felt shaky. "No, sweetie. Jon has to go back to Seattle. He has a job there and a family of his own."

Aubrey looked sad. "I'll miss him."

"So will I," she whispered, blinking harder. "But we'll be okay, Aubrey," she added bravely. "You and I are going to get along just fine. Maybe we'll get a pet. Would you like that?"

"Maybe," he said, cautious as ever about committing himself.

He was so much like Jerome in some ways, Amanda thought mistily. So much like herself in others. She and Aubrey *would* be fine, she thought with a renewed surge of hope. Eventually.

"Are you all right now?" she asked him, searching his face for any further misgivings. "Is there anything else you want to talk about tonight?"

He hesitated, then shook his head. "Not tonight."

"All right. Finish your homework and then get to bed, okay? I'll see you in the morning. Since it'll be Sunday and you don't have school and I don't have to go into the shop, let's plan to do something fun."

"Like what?" Aubrey asked, intrigued.

She kissed his forehead. "You be thinking about what you want to do and we'll discuss it at breakfast. Good night, Aubrey."

"Aunt Amanda?"

She was about to rise but paused. "Yes?"

"Would you mind calling me A.J.?"

She smiled. "No, A.J. I don't mind at all."

He returned the smile, looking happier than he had in a long time.

There was a lump in her throat when she left the room and closed the door behind her.

Jon's bedroom door was closed. She could hear him moving around inside. Tempted to go to him, she turned toward her own room, instead. She needed a few minutes to compose herself. Besides, she had a beautiful black nightgown he'd never seen. Maybe she'd slip into that before he joined her.

It seemed less and less likely that Amanda and Jon had any hope of a future together. As Eleanor had pointed out, Jon didn't fit into Amanda's life here. He was a Seattle cop, and he seemed perfectly happy with his life there. Amanda felt firmly rooted in Memphis. Her career was here and her family. Her first loyalty had to be to Aubrey. Having so recently lost his parents, and now so dependent on her, he needed a great deal of attention and reassurance, as she understood now. She wasn't sure she had time to be romantically involved with *anyone* now, carry on a career and still give Aubrey the time and attention he needed.

She told herself she shouldn't feel trapped. She was taking on this responsibility willingly. But still, she found herself blinking back tears at what might have been between her and Jon had things been different.

She forced back the last of the tears and defiantly pulled out the sheer black nightgown. She and Jon might not have a future ahead of them, but they had tonight.

She intended to make the best of it.

11

JON PAUSED outside Amanda's door, feeling foolishly as though he should be carrying something when he joined her. Flowers? Champagne? *Stupid*.

He was already half-aroused, tingling with anticipation of the night to come. When he went to tap on her door, he noticed that his hand wasn't quite steady. What the hell? No woman had ever made him tremble before.

He'd fallen hard and fast for Amanda Hightower, a woman who moved in circles far different from his own—geographically, economically and in nearly every other way. It was entirely possible that he was headed for heartache. Yet he didn't seem to be making any effort to protect himself. He hadn't even allowed himself to think beyond this night.

He didn't know what tomorrow would bring. But he had tonight. For now, that would have to be enough.

He tapped on the door.

"Come in." Amanda's voice was only a faint murmur, but he heard her clearly enough.

He turned the knob, stepped into the room—froze at the sight of her.

She was stunning. Her hair was loose and brushed to a soft, gleaming mane. Her dark eyes were wide and expressive, his own excitement mirrored in them. She wore something black and filmy that bared her sleek lightly tanned arms and dipped to show a tantalizing expanse of creamy cleavage. It clung to her small waist and then flared around her long slender legs. When she moved, the garment moved with her, caressing the parts of her it concealed. Jon's palms itched to touch those hidden treasures. And he would. Oh, yes, he most certainly would.

"You're beautiful," he said, his voice a low hoarse growl.

Her smile was ancient, mysterious, beckoning. "Thank you."

He moved closer to her, drawn by a force he couldn't have resisted if he'd tried. The faint scent of flowers tickled his nose, wafting from her flushed, freshly showered skin.

He reached out a hand and stroked the tips of his fingers down one delicate arm. *Mine*, he thought, the surge of possessiveness new to him, as were so many of the feelings she evoked in him. *At least for tonight.*

Ignoring the sudden ache in his chest, he reached out to pull her into his arms. He kissed her with all the tenderness, all the passion, all the wonder he was feeling, trying to convey without words that these emotions were special, different, more intense than anything he'd ever shared with anyone.

His rigid muscles quivered with the restraint he imposed on himself. All his instincts urged him to take her. Now. Hard. Fast.

He forced himself to go slowly, reminding himself that they had plenty of time. All night. And he wanted this to be the most perfect night either of them had ever known.

"Amanda," he murmured, just because he wanted to say her name. "I . . ."

But he didn't know what else to say, had no words to tell her how she made him feel. He contented himself with another long, soul-deep kiss, which she returned with a fervor that made his knees go weak.

He didn't know which of them made the first move toward the bed, who reached out first to rid them of the clothing that separated them. But then they were together, nude and warm and locked in each other's arms, the darkened room a cocoon of intimacy surrounding them, the bed a haven of privacy. Jon pressed his open mouth to the tip of one perfect breast and thought that if he died now, he'd have no complaints.

He spent a long time at her breasts, savoring their softness, their taste, their warmth and sweetness. Amanda gasped and arched beneath him; her fingers clutched at his hair, at his shoulders, urging him to hurry. He refused to be rushed and lingered until she grabbed his hand with a choked whimper of need and pushed it downward. Smiling against her hot damp skin, he relented and slid his fingers into the crisp wet curls between her legs, offering partial satisfaction with slow rhythmic strokes.

Amanda sighed her relief. Her lips racing over his face, she paused to kiss his temple, his brow, the tip of his nose, then caught his lower lip between her teeth and nipped his chin. He trapped her mouth beneath his own and plunged his tongue deep inside. And when neither of them could wait any longer, when both were in danger of going up in flames, he shifted between her raised knees and drove himself into her, joining them with a force that took their breath away, connecting them in a way that was much more than physical.

"Amanda," he murmured, his lips moving against hers. And her name was a song of love.

"TELL ME ABOUT YOUR DAY," he urged her a very long time later. They'd been lying snuggled together for hours, sometimes talking quietly, sometimes saying nothing, reaching out frequently to touch, to kiss, to savor the time. There'd been no talk of the future, no effort to label their feelings or define their wishes. There was no need for that tonight, Jon decided. They'd wait until daylight to face tomorrow.

Amanda groaned and buried her face in his shoulder. "You don't want to hear about my day," she assured him, her voice muffled.

"Yes, I do. What was so awful about it? Other than Worley's visit of course. I was here for that one."

She told him about Tricia's headache, late shipments, the disgruntlement of the few customers she did have. He rubbed her neck and kissed her in sympathy. He scowled when she described McFarland's behavior. "Did you call the police?"

"Yes. They made him leave."

"You might have to get a restraining order to keep him away."

"I hope he'll give up now. I've got enough to worry about right now without that."

"What else happened today?"

"I had lunch with Edward," she confessed somewhat hesitantly. "Before he came by here, apparently."

He scowled at the intrusion of her ex-fiancé's name. "Why?" he asked bluntly.

"He showed up without calling and announced that he was taking me to lunch. It seemed easier to go than to argue about it."

"What did he want?"

"*Not* that it's any of your business," she replied, softening the words with a faint smile, "but he wants to renew our relationship. I told him it was out of the question of course. The most Edward and I can ever be is friends—and I'm beginning to doubt that even that is possible. He has his nice qualities, but he can be very annoying, as well."

"He's a jerk."

She chuckled. "You're not exactly an objective observer. You and Edward didn't particularly take to one another when you met."

"Is that surprising? We both want the same woman."

His words seemed to fluster her. She cleared her throat. "Anyway, he took my rejection without causing a scene and left with a chaste kiss on the cheek. I'm not convinced he's given up entirely, but I think he's finally getting the hint that it's over between us."

"Just let me know if he starts making a nuisance of himself. I'll have a talk with him."

"You'll do no such thing. Besides," she added quietly, "you won't even be here. You'll be going back to Seattle Monday."

Jon didn't say anything. He wasn't sure he could force any words past the sudden lump in his throat.

"And then I came home and saw Howard's car," she continued with forced lightness. "You know the rest."

"Yeah. You aren't really worried about that clown taking you to court, are you? He doesn't have a prayer of getting custody of A.J., and I think he knows it."

"I'm worried about him causing more trouble," she admitted. "Aubrey,—I mean, A.J.—" she gave a weak smile smile, "—doesn't need more friction in his life. He's still getting over his parents' deaths, just learning to trust my feelings for him, finally starting to make friends and learn to play again. Howard makes him miserable, tells him things that upset him. I wish I could keep them apart."

"Then do it," Jon advised flatly. "You have no obligation to let Howard visit if his presence upsets the boy. Howard doesn't share custody, has no legal right to interfere in A.J.'s life. Tell him so. Better yet, have your lawyer tell him."

"Maybe I should. I thought it would be unfair to A.J. to keep him from his mother's only living relative. Now I'm beginning to think it would be better to do so. After all, my sister-in-law was never close to her brother. Wanda and Howard rarely saw each other. Howard's interest in his nephew has only developed since the accident."

"Since A.J. inherited his father's estate, you mean."

"I'm afraid so."

"Then cut the bastard off."

"I probably will—once everything settles down."

When will that be, Amanda? Where will you live? Will you ever think of me then? The questions trembled on his tongue, but he didn't voice them. *Tomorrow,* he reminded himself. Tomorrow was soon enough to face the future.

There were still several hours of tonight to enjoy.

JON DIDN'T KNOW what woke him sometime well after midnight. Maybe the awareness that he should get back to his own room before the household awoke, he decided, thinking without enthusiasm of the empty bed awaiting him. He glanced at Amanda, sleeping so soundly beside him, and considered curling up against her and going back to sleep. But if he did, there was always the chance he wouldn't wake again until late morning.

Better to go now, he thought with a sigh as he slid out of bed. Before he changed his mind.

Amanda didn't stir when he stepped into his clothes or when he let himself out of her room. He had already entered his own room and was reaching for the hem of his sweatshirt when something stopped him. He'd had bad feelings before, usually on the job, but this one was particularly strong. He wished he could understand it. Did it have to do with his impending separation from Amanda, or...?

He glanced at the doorway, thinking it wouldn't hurt to look in on the boy. The house was locked up tight of course—he'd made sure of that—but something told him he wouldn't get to sleep until he'd seen for himself that the kid was okay.

Shaking his head at his paranoia, he crossed the hallway and eased Aubrey's door open. A moment later he was across the room, staring down at the tousled, unmistakably empty bed.

Don't panic, he thought, whirling toward the bathroom. *The kid's here somewhere.*

He wasn't in the bathroom.

"The kitchen," Jon muttered, remembering the night the boy had surprised him and Amanda having their midnight snack.

Aubrey wasn't in the kitchen, either. Nor the den, nor anywhere else Jon looked in a preliminary search of the house. And worse, the security system that Jon had activated himself had been turned off. The front door wasn't even locked.

Cursing beneath his breath, Jon bolted up the stairs. He shook Amanda awake with more impatience than consideration.

Knuckling her eyes like a child, she groaned and squinted up at him. "What time is it? What's wrong?"

"It's 2:00 a.m. Aubrey's missing."

"*What?*" Sitting up, she clutched his arm. "Are you sure?"

"I'm sure," he answered grimly, wishing he'd known how to be more tactful with the news. "His bed's empty. The alarm system's been turned off and the front door's unlocked. I'm going out to check the grounds. You check the house again—I haven't looked in your mother's rooms—and if you don't find him, call the police."

Amanda was already throwing on some clothes. She was pale and shaken, but composed. Jon wished he had time to comfort her with a hug, but right now, Aubrey was his first concern.

It was a cloudy cool night. Jon's small flashlight had little effect on the deep shadows outside the range of the security lighting, but enough for him to determine that the boy didn't seem to be on the grounds. If he was, he was well hidden, but why would he be hiding? Jon had to assume that he wasn't on the grounds. That he'd been taken away.

The front gates were still closed and locked. The automatic opener that had been installed was efficient, but not soundless. Even if whoever had taken Aubrey had been in possession of an opener, the chances were slim he'd have gotten onto the grounds without Jon hearing. So how...?

He frowned as he looked toward the back of the estate in the direction of the creek that was hidden by trees even in daylight. A sudden memory flashed through his mind—Aubrey and Nathan running from there after their brief disappearance.

"Damn!" Jon muttered, slamming a fist into his other palm. He'd been an idiot, assuming for some reason that the boys had left the grounds through the front gate. They'd come from the back of the estate, not the front. And Jon had been too wrapped up in his convoluted feelings for Amanda to let the significance of that sink in.

Amanda was just hanging up the telephone in the front parlor when Jon returned to the house. Eleanor stood nearby in a long satin dressing gown and slippers, not a gray hair out of place, no sign of turmoil on her face except for the light lines around her unpainted mouth. "I called the police," Amanda said. "Aubrey's not in the house."

Jon nodded. "Not on the grounds, either—at least, not as far as I could tell. Do you know Terry's home number?"

"Yes. Why?"

"Dial it." He stepped close to the telephone, prepared to take it from her when she'd finished dialing.

Amanda didn't question him again, but obligingly punched in the seven digits before handing the receiver to Jon.

A woman's sleepy voice answered on the third ring. Her hello conveyed the slight panic most people feel at being called in the middle of the night.

Jon asked to speak to Terry, heard a rustle and a man's voice growl a question, and then Terry was on the line, sounding wide awake. "Jon? What's happened?"

"A.J.'s missing. Someone got through the system—with a key and the security codes apparently."

There was a taut pause and then Terry said, "I didn't have anything to do with this, Jon."

"Hell, I know that," Jon answered impatiently. The thought had never crossed his mind, though he realized it probably should have. Other than Jon and the members of the immediate family, Terry and Roseanne were the only ones who had a key and knowledge of the code. Eleanor had insisted on showing them that trust. Having spent nearly a week with them, Jon didn't doubt either of them.

"I need to know how the boys got out of the grounds yesterday afternoon," he explained. "The front gate's still locked. Someone had to have gotten in another way."

"I don't know," Terry said, relieved by Jon's unquestioning trust but puzzled by the question. "I just assumed they went through the gate. It was open most of the afternoon."

"Yeah, I thought the same thing," Jon agreed." But I've just remembered that they were coming from the back of the grounds, not the front, when we spotted them."

"Hang on a minute. I'll go ask Nathan."

Keeping the receiver to his ear, Jon glanced at Amanda. "The cops'll be here soon. Go ahead and open the gates for them." He didn't want any more time wasted than absolutely necessary.

She nodded and moved away just as Terry came back on the line. "There's an opening in the brick wall on the east corner of the estate," he said grimly. "It's hidden by bushes and vines, but Aubrey has apparently known about it for some time. He showed it to Nathan. I'm on my way, Jon."

Jon didn't try to dissuade him. They could use his help. "Thanks, Terry."

THE SAME TWO OFFICERS who'd responded to the intruder call earlier that week arrived only moments after Jon hung up the phone. They immediately went into conference with Jon—almost, Amanda thought, as though he was a member of their own team, rather than just a visitor to their town. Sick with worry and futile self-reproach, she paced the parlor while Jon and the police officers talked, her mind spinning with questions and fears. Was she going to lose Aubrey so soon after finally breaking through to him?

Wearing hastily donned jeans, a sweatshirt and a pair of sneakers, Terrence arrived not long after the policemen. They immediately began to question him, suspicion written all over their faces, but Jon's defense of the chauffeur seemed to convince the officers of Terrence's loyalty to the family.

"No one heard anything?" one of the policeman—the younger one, whose badge identified him as Murphy—asked.

Amanda and Eleanor shook their heads. "Neither did I," Jon said with a twist of self-disgust to his mouth. Amanda knew he would be blaming himself for this. She wanted to reassure him that he'd done all he could, that no one could possibly blame him, but she kept quiet, knowing he wouldn't appreciate her defending him in front of the others.

"I'm certain Howard Worley has something to do with this," Eleanor announced, her faded eyes sparking with fury at the possibility. "I insist you send someone there to question him immediately."

That, of course, made an explanation necessary. When he heard of Worley's threats that afternoon, Murphy agreed that Worley was a suspect. He called in a request for a car to be sent to question Worley regarding Aubrey's disappearance. Not, he added, that anything could really be done until they had more to go on—a ransom call or note, some proof that the boy hadn't run away. He assured them hastily that he believed them that Aubrey wouldn't have done anything of the sort, but his superiors might not be so sure. After all, kids ran away all the time.

"Not this one," Jon said, frustration evident in the hard set of his jaw.

"You're sure the security system was on?" Murphy asked after a moment of silence, phrasing the question carefully—probably in deference to Jon's barely suppressed fury with the entire situation.

"Positive. I set it myself," Jon answered flatly.

Both the officers seemed to think that settled any doubt. "So someone—Worley or whoever—had a key," the other officer, Catlett, said.

"Apparently," Jon agreed. "And the four-digit security code."

"Who has keys to the system?"

"Mother and I do," Amanda replied. "Terrence and our housekeeper, Roseanne Wallace. There's also a spare that Jon's been using."

"Let's see all the keys," Murphy suggested. "Someone call the housekeeper and make sure she knows where hers is."

"I'll call her," Eleanor offered, rising stiffly. "Terrence, my key is in the drawer of the cherry table in the entryway. Would you get it, please?"

Amanda had expected to find her own keys in her purse, which should have been on the small desk in her room. It wasn't. Frowning, she tried to remember what she'd done with it. The jacket she'd worn to work was slung over the desk chair. Her car keys were in the pocket, where she'd carelessly left them. But where had she put her purse?

Ten minutes later she had to admit the purse was missing. "My key is in it," she added, twisting her hands as she faced the questioning crowd in the parlor. "Wherever it is."

"Then your key is the only one unaccounted for," Jon muttered. "Damn. When did you last see your purse?"

"I don't remember."

"Think, Amanda. Did you have it when you left your shop?"

"I'm *trying* to think!" she snapped, raising her hands to her temples. And then she took a deep breath. "Sorry. I . . ."

"I know." Jon squeezed her shoulder. "And I know you're trying. Picture yourself leaving your shop, Amanda. Did you have your purse?"

She could see her hand on the door, could see herself locking it with the shop key on the same ring as her car keys. She'd carried her jacket over her arm. Had the purse been beneath it?

"I know I had it when I went to lunch with Edward," she mused aloud, remembering that she'd freshened her lipstick before returning to work. "But after that . . . I wonder if I left it in his car. I was rather in a hurry."

"He came here after lunch," she remembered, turning to her mother. "He didn't mention that he was returning my purse or anything like that, did he?"

"No. He never even mentioned that you'd lunched with him," Eleanor replied, her disapproval of Amanda's actions evident. "But isn't it just as likely that Howard could have taken the purse during the confusion when we were looking for Aubrey and Terrence's son this afternoon?"

"It's very possible," Jon agreed grimly. "If he's home, he'll be questioned, Eleanor. If he's not . . ." He let the sentence fade out, since they all knew what Howard's absence would imply.

"It's also possible that someone took the purse from my office at the shop," Amanda felt compelled to point out. "Or it could still be sitting beneath my desk, where I always keep it. As I said, I really can't remember when I saw it last."

"We'll go check the shop," Jon said, welcoming an excuse to take some sort of action. "No need for us to hang around here, is there, officers?"

"Even if someone snatched the purse and got hold of the keys," Terrence interjected thoughtfully, "what about the security code? How could they know that? Have either Worley or Miller seen you enter the digits, Aman—er, Miss Hightower?"

"Amanda," she corrected him, ashamed that she'd never asked him to call her that before. He'd been almost a member of the family for ten years. How could she have been so thoughtless? "And, no. I never operated the security system in front of either of them."

"You wouldn't have had the code written down anywhere in your purse, would you?" Jon asked, although he thought the possibility was almost too ridiculous even to propose.

Amanda cleared her throat.

Jon's eyes narrowed. "You didn't, did you? Tell me you weren't that careless."

"I can't remember numbers," she protested. "Everyone knows that about me—it's some sort of mental block I've got. I keep all the numbers I need to remember written beside fictitious names in my address book. No one would know what they were just by glancing through it. They'd assume the numbers were addresses and telephone numbers. Edward—" She stopped, then began again more slowly, "Edward suggested the system to me over a year ago. It seemed like a very good idea."

Jon moved toward the door. "Let's go. Bring the keys to your shop. We'll stop there first."

"Detective Luck," Officer Catlett said quickly, "don't forget you're out of your jurisdiction here. Why don't you let us handle this?"

"Just going for a drive, Officer," Jon replied blandly. "Terry, you'll stay here with Eleanor? Be prepared to take any calls. We'll be checking in frequently."

"I'll be here."

"Good."

Ignoring sputtered protests from Eleanor and halfhearted remonstrations from the police officers, who were already being summoned by radio to respond to other calls, Jon towed Amanda out of the house without giving her a chance to object. Not that she would have, anyway. Like Jon, she felt the need to do something, *anything*, rather than sit and wait for word of her nephew's whereabouts.

AMANDA'S PURSE wasn't in her desk, or anywhere else in her shop. Jon didn't want to linger there.

"I think we'll pay a little visit to your ex-fiancé," he said as they left the shop.

"You can't possibly believe Edward has kidnapped Aubrey," Amanda said, snapping herself into the driver's seat of her car while Jon settled into the passenger side. "He can be snobbish and annoying at times, but he's not cut out for this sort of thing, and why on earth would he do something like this, anyway?"

"Why don't we ask him?" Jon motioned toward the steering wheel. "Drive."

She was too worried about her nephew to feel much resentment for Jon's very officious behavior since he'd woken her to tell her Aubrey was missing. But, she thought grimly, turning the car in the direction of Edward's apartment, as soon as this was all over, and Aubrey was safe . . .

Oh, please, God, let Aubrey be safe.

AMANDA COULDN'T RESIST giving Jon an I-told-you-so look when Edward answered his door, sleepy-eyed and tousled and obviously just roused from his bed. Knotting a bathrobe over his cotton pajamas, he looked from Amanda to Jon with a puzzled frown.

"Amanda? What in the world..."

Torn between relief that Edward apparently had nothing to do with her nephew's disappearance and sick with fear for Aubrey's safety, Amanda tried to explain. "Aubrey's missing, Edward. We think someone got in the house using my keys. I've lost my purse, and I thought it was possible that I'd left it in your car at lunch."

"Aubrey's missing?" Edward repeated, looking shocked. "Poor Amanda, you must be frantic. Come in. Both of you."

"We can't stay," Amanda explained, though she stepped inside the apartment. Jon silently followed and closed the door behind them. "We have to look for Aubrey. I was just hoping you'd remember seeing my purse after we returned from lunch."

"No," he answered apologetically. "I'm afraid I didn't notice your purse—or lack of one. I was concentrating solely on you, Amanda."

Jon made a sound deep in his throat and Amanda gave him a quick glance of warning. He stood beside the antique coat tree next to the door, his hands buried in the pockets of the jacket he'd donned over his gray running suit, his face hard and expressionless.

"I'm sorry we disturbed you, Edward," she said. "We'd better be going now."

"You will let me know if you hear anything about your nephew?"

"Of course I will."

"Are you sure there's nothing else I can do?"

She shook her head and took a step toward the door, impatient to be gone. "No, but thank you for offering."

Edward put a hand on her shoulder, his face close to hers. "Amanda, darling, I can see how terribly you're suffering. It tears me apart to see you like this. Isn't there anything . . . ?"

A crash from behind them made Amanda whirl around. Jon had stumbled into the coatrack, though she didn't know whether he'd done so because his bad leg had thrown him off balance or because he'd wanted to interrupt Edward's concerned speech. The coat tree had fallen to the floor, the raincoat and blazer it had held tangled around it. "Sorry, Miller," Jon said casually, reaching toward the mess. "Clumsy of me."

"I'll take care of it," Edward said, making a hasty move in that direction.

Jon had already grabbed the blazer by the hem and held it upside down as he lifted it from the floor. Something hit the polished wood floor with a soft thud.

Amanda stared uncertainly. "Edward? What are you doing with my address book?"

And then she gasped and spun to face him, feeling the blood drain from her face. "Edward!"

He made a move that was probably an attempt to run, but he didn't get more than three steps. Jon brought him down with a flying tackle that couldn't have been good for his injured leg. Still stunned by the implications of finding her address book in Edward's possession, Amanda watched in dismay as Edward struck out, desperation giving him strength. The fight was brutal, but in a mercifully short time Jon was sitting astride Edward's chest, his hands around the other man's throat. Jon was breathing hard and an ugly bruise was beginning to darken on his cheek, but he was totally in control of the situation when he asked, "Where's the boy, Miller?"

"I don't know what you're talking about," Edward blustered, squirming beneath Jon's weight and gasping for breath.

His hands still gripping Edward's throat, Jon lifted the man's head and smashed it against the wooden floor. Edward screamed with pain and Amanda cried out in protest. Jon ignored her, his eyes focused with deadly intent on Edward's face, which was rapidly turning red from the pressure of Jon's fingers against his windpipe.

"*Where is he?*" Jon asked again, and his voice was so deadly that Amanda shivered at the sound of it.

Edward reacted in much the same manner. "He hasn't been harmed," he choked out, clawing at Jon's white-knuckled hands. "For God's sake, Amanda, get him off me!"

Amanda took a deep breath and stepped closer. "Where's Aubrey, Edward? What have you done with him?"

"I'll tell you, I swear. Just call him off."

Amanda placed a hand on Jon's iron-hard shoulder. "Ease off enough to let him speak, Jon," she advised quietly. "If he doesn't tell us everything we want to know, then you can do whatever you want to him."

Edward's eyes widened in panic and disbelief at her callousness. After that, he couldn't speak quickly enough.

Amanda had been right in one respect. Edward really wasn't cut out for this sort of thing.

As LONG AS HE LIVED Jon would never forget the look on Aubrey's face when the police burst into the run-down shack in western Memphis where the boy was being held. The cops had insisted that Amanda stay behind until the kidnappers were safely apprehended, but they were unable to convince Jon to remain in the car. Fortunately the man and woman who'd been holding Aubrey were taken without difficulty, though they loudly protested their innocence. Aubrey, still dressed in pajamas, burst into tears of relief and threw himself into Jon's arms.

Amanda hurried inside the moment she was given permission. "Aubrey!" she cried, her cheeks wet with tears.

Without hesitation, Aubrey pulled himself out of Jon's arms and fell into his aunt's fierce embrace. Touched at the emotion visible between the two, Jon stood close by, trying hard to overlook the way his leg was throbbing.

He'd felt something tear when he'd thrown himself onto Miller. He'd hoped the pain would subside if he ignored it long enough. Instead, it was getting worse. Clenching his teeth to hold back a groan, he told himself he didn't have time to worry about the pain. The kid was more important at the moment.

"You're sure you're okay, A.J.?" he asked, placing a hand on the boy's thin shoulder. "They didn't hurt you?"

"I have a headache," Aubrey admitted. "The man who got me out of bed put something over my face that knocked me out. When I woke up, I was here, and those two were standing over me. But I *knew* you'd find me," he added. The fervent confidence in his voice brought a lump to Jon's throat.

"We're taking you home now, Aubrey," Amanda assured the boy. She was unable to release him, needing the contact to reassure herself that he was back with her. "No one will ever do this to you again."

With a tearful glance at Jon, she turned and started to lead the boy toward the door.

Jon tried to follow. He managed two steps before his leg collapsed beneath him in a fiery explosion of pain.

PROPPED AGAINST the headboard of the bed in his room at the Hightower home, Jon stared glumly at the brace that immobilized his right leg from midthigh to ankle. Felling Edward Miller with a flying tackle on a hardwood floor hadn't been the smartest move he'd ever made. He'd spent two nights in a Memphis hospital having repairs made to his reinjured ligaments before being released to recuperate for a few days with the Hightowers.

He'd have to start using that damned cane again, he thought grimly, glaring at the brace. He'd be leaving Memphis in the same shape in which he'd arrived— worse, actually. His heart, at least, had been intact when he'd left Seattle.

The man arrested in the shack had been the one who'd taken the boy, his wife the woman who'd approached Aubrey at the library. An experienced burglar who'd only recently been released from prison— after robbing a branch of the bank Amanda's grandfather had started so many years ago—the kidnapper had deftly bypassed the security systems once he'd been provided with a key and the code from Amanda's address book. Aubrey had been drugged and carried out through the opening in the brick wall that had been the one vulnerable area in the estate's new security system.

Aubrey said he'd known about the opening for weeks, but hadn't thought to mention it to anyone— another indication of how poor communication had been in the Hightower household for the past five months, Jon thought with a twist of his mouth.

Edward Miller, who was also in jail, blamed Amanda for his participation in the kidnapping. She'd led him on, he claimed bitterly. Promised to marry him. Let him believe he'd never have to worry about money again. It was her fault that he'd run up so many bills in anticipation of his good fortune. Her fault that without her he now had no way of paying those bills, that his reputation and credibility at the university would suffer as a result. When he'd been approached by the would-be kidnappers, who knew about his broken engagement, he hadn't been able to turn down their proposition that he help them in their scheme.

He never would have hurt the boy, he virtuously assured anyone who would listen. He only wanted what he considered his due for all the months he'd spent courting Amanda and supporting her, with encouragement and advice and affection, during her early days in the retail business. offering encouragement and advice and affection. Just enough to cover his debts, pay off the couple who'd actually kidnapped the boy—and maybe just a little extra to set aside. A university professor, even a well-respected one, didn't make a great deal of money, he pointed out resentfully. And he'd always liked the things that a great deal of money could buy.

Now it was Thursday evening, five days after Aubrey's rescue, and Jon had been pampered and treated like an injured hero ever since. Restoring Aubrey Hightower to the loving arms of his family had ensured Jon a place of honor in this household, but damned if he hadn't been more comfortable when he'd just been a guest who didn't fit in very well with his elegant surroundings.

Jon still found it hard not to blame himself for part of Aubrey's ordeal. If only he'd thought to check the entire wall around the estate. If only he'd been in his own room that night with the door open to allow him to keep watch over Aubrey. If only he hadn't been so thoroughly bewitched by Amanda that he couldn't concentrate on the real reason he'd come to Memphis in the first place.

He'd blown it, big time. Thank God it had all worked out satisfactorily, though even that lucky break with the address book had been as much by accident as by design.

A tap on his door made him look up suspiciously. If that was Roseanne carrying another tray of goodies she'd baked just for him, or his mother, who'd arrived in Memphis the day after Aubrey's rescue and had been having a wonderful time ever since visiting her friend and hovering over her wounded-hero son, or worse, Eleanor, with her awkward solicitousness and stilted gratitude....

"Who is it?"

"Amanda."

He relaxed. "Come in."

She opened the door and peeked in a bit uncertainly. He'd made it quite clear earlier that he'd needed time to himself.

He motioned her in. "Quick, come in and close the door before someone follows you."

With a smile, she closed the door, came close to the bed and paused there with her hands clasped loosely in front of her. It was the first time they'd been alone together since he'd left her bed in the wee hours of Sunday morning.

"How's A.J.?" he asked to distract himself from the memories of everything that had occurred before he'd left her bed.

"He's fine," she assured him. "He and Nathan are downstairs playing a video game in the den. I didn't even know Aubrey had a video game."

Jon thought of the black plastic box he'd spotted beneath the bed on his first day here, but didn't mention it. "Sit down. You look done in."

She perched on the edge of the bed and sighed. "I am a little tired," she admitted. "It's been a long day."

"Tell me about it."

"Is your leg hurting?"

"No," he lied. "Don't worry about it."

She gave him a faint smile. "You wouldn't tell me if it was hurting you, would you?"

"No," he admitted, returning the smile, pleased to see that the stricken look she'd had in her eyes the past few days was gone.

"Hopelessly macho."

"Hopelessly," he agreed, reaching for her hand.

She twined her fingers with his. "I can't forget that you injured yourself saving Aubrey. I know you're tired of hearing this, but I have to say it again. Thank you, Jon, for everything."

"You're welcome," he answered shortly. "Now change the subject."

Her smile was tremulous but genuine. "What would you like to talk about?"

"Us."

The smile wavered. "Us?" Her voice had risen half an octave. She cleared her throat before speaking again. "What about us?"

"If you think I'm going to go back to Seattle in a couple of days and forget all about you, you're crazy," he said bluntly, recklessly. "I've been looking for someone like you all my life, Amanda Hightower. Now that I've found you, I'm not about to let you get away."

Her fingers had gone slack in his. He hoped it was due to surprise rather than resistance.

"Well?" he prodded, when she didn't respond. A surge of uneasiness coursed through him, and he felt the urge to grab her and tell her that she might as well accept that he would never—*could* never—let her go. She was his, dammit. Had been from the first time he'd taken her into his arms.

"I . . . don't know what you want me to say."

"You could begin by telling me you don't want me to leave and forget about you."

She blinked, and he thought he saw a sheen of tears in her dark eyes. Regret? His chest tightened. "Amanda?"

"I don't want you to leave," she whispered, dropping her gaze so that her expression was hidden from him. "I don't think I could ever want you to leave. But . . ."

Relief made him light-headed. His fingers tightened around hers. "I love you," he blurted—words he hadn't said to a woman in a very long time. Words he'd never meant the way he meant them now. "I think I have from that first day."

Her eyes were swimming now. He couldn't tell if they were tears of joy or sadness. "You don't even know me," she managed, her voice choked. "It hasn't even been two weeks."

"I know all I need to know. I'm not a kid, Amanda. I know what I want. I want you. A future with you. A family."

"But what about Aubrey—A.J.? I have to put him first, Jon. Surely you understand that."

"In case you haven't noticed, I'm crazy about that little genius of a nephew of yours, Amanda Hightower. The proposal includes both of you."

"Proposal?" she whispered.

"As in marriage. Sharing living quarters. Double rings and baby carriages."

She gulped, audibly.

Starting to panic again, Jon gripped her hand until her knuckles turned white. "Look, I know this has been quick. I know you haven't had any time to think— Oh, hell, I've really made a mess of this, haven't I? I'll give you time, Amanda. Court you long-distance, move to Memphis, do whatever I have to do. I just know I can't tell you goodbye."

"Jon, I—"

"Jon? Are you— Oh. Sorry, I'll come back later." Aubrey started to withdraw from the partially opened door. Jon hadn't even heard the door open, and neither had Amanda, apparently.

"No, it's okay," he said quickly, motioning the boy in. "Don't leave."

"I should have knocked," Aubrey apologized. His eyes moved searchingly from Jon to Amanda. "But Nathan went home and I wanted to see if you were okay, and I forgot."

"It's okay," Jon repeated. "C'mere."

Aubrey approached the bed, still studying their serious faces. "Is something wrong?"

"I just proposed to your aunt," Jon answered rashly. "What do you think of that?"

Amanda choked. Aubrey's eyes widened. "Proposed? Marriage?"

"That's right. You have any objections?"

"No, sir!" Aubrey answered, his eyes shining. "That would make you my uncle. I'd like that a lot."

"So would I," Jon assured him gently, his fingers still wrapped tightly around Amanda's icy ones. "I was just waiting for an answer."

Aubrey turned to his aunt, looking astonished that she hadn't accepted immediately. "You don't *want* to marry Jon?"

Amanda took a deep breath, her gaze locking with Jon's. "Yes," she said, her voice quiet and sincere. "I want very much to marry Jon. But—"

"You're worried about me, aren't you?" Aubrey interrupted, looking stricken. "You don't have to be, Aunt Amanda. I promise I won't be any trouble. Especially," he added, his thin shoulders slumping, "after I leave for boarding school next year."

"Boarding school?" Jon repeated incredulously. "What makes you think you'll be going to boarding school next year?"

Aubrey cleared his throat and looked down at his shoes. "That's what my father wanted me to do. There's a school in Maryland for gifted and talented kids, and my dad planned to send me there when I turned ten. I heard Grandmother say that she and Aunt Amanda would stick with the curriculum my parents had worked out for me."

Jon glared at Amanda. "You'd really do that?"

"Of course not," she answered heatedly. "Not if Au— A.J. doesn't want to go. I knew about my brother's plans of course, but I'd always intended to consult A.J. before I committed to anything like that. I'd hoped he'd prefer to stay with me, instead."

His face lighting, Aubrey looked up. "Does that mean I don't have to go if I don't want to? I can stay with you and Jon?"

Amanda reached out her free hand to him. "Of course you can, darling! Oh, Aubrey, have you been worrying that I might send you away?"

He nodded. "Uncle Howard said I'd only be in your way if you ever wanted to start your own family. He said you probably couldn't wait to send me off to school."

"Your uncle Howard is full of it," Amanda told him flatly.

Aubrey grinned.

"She's right, he is," Jon seconded. "And you won't ever have to worry about him again once the three of us move to Seattle."

"We're moving to Seattle? What about Grandmother? And Aunt Amanda's shop?"

Jon looked at Amanda. "Maybe we'll end up staying in Memphis," he revised, aware he'd been guilty of making some rather sweeping assumptions. "I can always get a job with the police force here, if that's what we decide to do. But I think your grandmother would get along just fine if we did move, and your aunt could open a new shop in Seattle. We'll talk about all the options before we make any decisions. All three of us. The way families are supposed to talk."

Aubrey nodded happily. "I think I'd like Seattle."

"I'm sure you would. But we'll discuss it later. Right now, why don't you go see if Roseanne would sneak you a cookie or something. And take your time about it," Jon suggested with a wink.

The boy grinned, looking happier than Jon had ever seen him. He leaned impulsively over the bed to give Jon a hug. "See you later, Uncle Jon," he said, then dashed out of the room before Jon could respond.

Jon cleared his throat of the huge lump that had formed there. "I really like that kid."

"So do I," Amanda said shakily, wiping her eyes with her fingertips.

Jon tugged her downward, bringing her face close to his. "Amanda? You're sure about this? I haven't forced you into something you aren't ready for?"

"I love you, Jonathan Luck," she murmured, and his heart leapt in response to the words he'd wanted so badly to hear. "I want to marry you. You haven't forced me into anything."

"How's your mother going to feel about it?"

"Ever since you rescued Aubrey, my mother has been all but pushing me into your arms. She thinks you're a hero."

He squirmed in embarrassment against the headboard. "Hardly that. But I'll be a good husband to you and a good father to A.J. and the other kids we may have. I swear it."

"I know you will."

He pulled her hungrily into his arms. "How did I ever get this lucky?" he muttered before covering her mouth with his own.

It was a long time later before he lifted his head with a groan. "Oh, no."

Her eyes shining, her lips damp and smiling, Amanda lay in his arms and looked curiously up at him. "What is it?"

"Looks like I owe my mother another favor. Heaven only knows what she'll expect from me now."

She laughed at his glum tone. "If it makes you feel any better, I owe her a few, myself, for sending you to Memphis."

"Don't think she won't point that out."

Still smiling, Amanda pulled his head back down to hers. "We won't worry about it. I doubt she'd ever ask more than we'd be willing to give."

Enthusiastically returning her kiss, Jon decided to wait until after he and Amanda were married to explain a few things about his mother. He didn't want to push his luck.